BAKEMONO

EMMA BOWERS

Bakemono is a Japanese term for *monster*.
Baka na mono is just *something stupid*.

*To all of the YouTubers who kept
me sane during the pandemic.*

*And to my wonderful son for helping me
during the creative process for this book.*

CONTENTS

1.	Ghost Hunt	1
2.	Oni	11
3.	Hellfire Dante	21
4.	Japan	29
5.	Road Trip	37
6.	Yamanaka Inn	47
7.	On	55
8.	Déjà Vu	65
9.	Yokai	75
10.	Danger	83
11.	No Signal	89
12.	Nightmare	97
13.	Sweetheart	107
14.	Run	115
15.	Found Footage	123
16.	Fix It in Post	131
	Epilogue: Life After Death	135
	About the Author	139

ONE

GHOST HUNT

GHOST HUNT MISSION OBJECTIVES:

1. *Gather three pieces of evidence and correctly identify ghost type (Reward: $100)*
2. *Witness a haunting event (Reward: $10)*
3. *Capture a picture of the ghost (Reward: $25)*
4. *Find and cleanse the cursed item with a smudge stick (Reward: $50)*
5. *Successfully banish the ghost (Reward: $75)*

In a military-size canvas tent outside an abandoned orphanage somewhere in Wisconsin, Dante Anderson scanned through the mission objectives on the whiteboard a second time. Although this was only his third mission with the team, he was starting to notice a pattern with the objectives. Eyeing the fifth objective, he chewed on his bottom lip in frustration. "Hey," he spoke in a hushed voice to his friend, Damien, standing next to him. "Can you show me how to banish the ghost this time?"

Damien chuckled. "Do you hate being the newb that much?" His friendly Estuary English accent did nothing to ease the sting of hearing the truth. Dante pouted in response, causing Damien to backtrack. "Look, just stick with being the photographer for now... At least until you get more experience."

Dante was about to complain when another one of his friends, Mikey, interrupted. "We could have Dante be in charge of the spirit box this time," he offered. Aside from photographer duty, the spirit box was one of the easier tasks for new hunters and could be done without getting in the way of the others.

The fourth friend of the group, Andy, laughed. "Don't listen to him, Dante! Using the spirit box tends to attract attention from the ghost. Mikey just doesn't want to risk dying."

"No one wants to die!" Mikey whined. Out of the group, Mikey and Andy had the most ghost-hunting experience, but that didn't mean they agreed on hunting strategies. The two bickered about what would be the best task to assign to Dante.

"Whatever," Dante finally decided for himself, picking up a device that looked like a handheld radio. "I'll be spirit box guy this time."

Damien grabbed a smudge stick and infrared thermometer. Andy picked up a crucifix and EMF reader. Finally, Mikey took a camera and a UV light.

Geared up, the four friends left the safety of their tent and walked out into the dark night. The group approached the iron fence in front of the orphanage. A weathered plaque barely hung on to the fence, reading, HOPECREST, FOUNDED 1908. The rusted gate opened with a long, loud groan that reminded Dante of the roar of a Japanese *kaiju* monster. The concrete stairs leading up to the two-story building were crumbling to the point that it was a wonder they could hold any weight without falling apart. At the top of the stairs was a multi-paneled wooden door that had splintered and cracked in one of the lower corners. The white paint that coated the door had faded to a dingy yellow that chipped as the door creaked open.

Inside the narrow lobby, ominous silence greeted the group. Even carrying flashlights, they could barely see anything that wasn't right in front of their faces. Andy checked his map in the back of his instruction manual. "Okay, although this place is pretty large, it's actually just a big square. In the middle is a courtyard with a playground. Although the ghost shouldn't appear out there, you can use it as a shortcut to get across the building quicker on the ground floor."

"And if the ghost is on the second floor?" Damien asked. This was his first mission at the orphanage.

"Either hide or try to lap it until you can get downstairs," Andy answered. Putting his map away, he turned to the group. "But for now, Dante and Damien will take the ground floor, and Mikey and I will take the second floor. As soon as any of you come across anything suspicious, contact everyone on your radio." He pressed the button on his radio and his voice came through with a crackle of static. "Understood?"

Dante, Damien, and Mikey pressed the buttons on their radios and replied in unison, "Understood!"

After checking around in the headmaster's office off the right side of the entrance lobby, Dante and Damien found glass French doors that led to an overgrown courtyard. The outline of a dilapidated playground was barely visible in the cloud-covered moonlight. Just as they were about to split up, Mikey's voice came over the radio: "Hey, guys! Come here. I think I've found something. Up the stairs and to the left at the back corner of the building."

"We'll be right there," Damien replied into the radio. He and Dante trudged up the staircase to the second floor. As the two friends turned the corner upstairs, they saw a flashlight flicker on and off at the end of the hall.

"Down here, guys!" Mikey yelled, his voice echoing down the hallway. "It's in this room." Dante and Damien peeked into the room from the entrance. It was in a sad state, with only one twin-size metal spring bed in the corner and an old-fashioned oak wardrobe in another. Andy was already in the room, walking around with the

EMF reader. "I found claw marks on the back of the door," Mikey explained, and flashed his UV light at the door to reveal green scratches.

"Good job, mate," Damien said with a smile. "Did you take a picture already?"

"Yeah, it should be in the book now," Mikey replied proudly.

"So we put that in the book as evidence, right?" Dante asked no one in particular. He opened his book to the page titled "Evidence" and looked at the list. Finding "claw marks," he checked the box next to it. Immediately three of the twelve types of ghosts became grayed out on the next page.

"Yeah, I'm not getting any EMF readings." In frustration, Andy tossed the machine onto the mold-stained, blue-striped mattress. "I'm going to head back to the tent and grab a journal."

"Wait, I'll come with you," Damien told him. "I'm not getting any freezing temps either." He was about to leave the room when he turned to Dante. "Hey, try using the spirit box to talk to it. The ghost's name is Robert Thomas."

Taking a deep breath, Dante pulled out the device and switched on the dial on top. A low hum came from the device, signaling it was on. "Robert Thomas, are you here?" Dante said in his clear, bass voice. There was no response. "Robert Thomas, give us a sign." Still no response. Annoyed, Dante tried to speak to the ghost again. "Robert Thomas, are you an asshole?"

Mikey burst into laughter while picking up the thermometer Damien had left. Laughter came over the radio from Damien and Andy as well. Encouraged by his friends, Dante continued to taunt the ghost. "Robert Thomas, do you like to eat ass?"

The spirit box suddenly replied with a deep, hollow, disembodied voice: "*Die.*"

"What did it say? Did it tell me to die?" Dante asked. When Mikey nodded, Dante dramatically threw the spirit box onto the bed. "Shut up, Rob Thomas!" At that moment, a distorted crackle came over the group radio and the flashlights flickered on and off. "Are you doing that?" Dante asked Mikey.

"No..." Mikey replied with some uncertainty. Then he jumped. "It's hunting! Hide!"

Dante was about to step outside the room when the door slammed shut in his face and locked. "What the hell?" he exclaimed. He tried to open the door, but it wouldn't budge. "Why isn't this opening?" he cried in panic. He looked back over his shoulder to ask his friend what he should do. It took him a moment to realize an invisible force was holding Mikey up by the neck.

"Oh, come on!" Mikey whined. "Dante was the one with the spirit box!" Then his head turned at an odd angle until his neck snapped. Dante covered his mouth in shock as Mikey's body was tossed across the room like a ragdoll. The force of impact caused his head to become stuck in the wall, leaving the rest of his body hanging out in an awkward position.

The lights stopped flickering, and the door clicked open. *Fuck this!* Dante thought, immediately leaving the room. He wanted to run, but his body was moving extremely slowly. It reminded him of the nightmares he'd had as a kid when he was running in slow motion while trying to escape monsters. He reached the stairs and the group radio returned to normal.

Andy's calm voice came over the radio. "Mikey, Dante, are you guys okay?"

Dante pressed the button on his radio. "Mikey's dead!" Then he growled, "How the hell are you so calm?!"

"Hey, chill, man. It'll be all right," Andy's voice echoed up from the bottom of the stairs. Neither his face nor his voice showed any emotion, despite their friend having just been killed by a ghost. "So we confirmed the spirit box as evidence. Did you get a picture of Mikey's corpse?"

"No, he had the camera," Dante replied as he checked off "spirit box" on the evidence page. Another three ghost types were grayed out on the other page. He shook his head. "Wait, why the hell would I want a picture of that?"

"It counts toward the 'witness a haunting event' objective," Damien explained. He was following Andy up the stairs with a container of salt in his hand. "You should probably head back to the tent, Dante. Your heart rate is extremely high."

"I'm fine! I can handle it," Dante replied, still obviously shaken from Mikey's death.

"Nah, man," Andy replied over the radio while walking

back toward the room. "If your heart rate gets too high, you die. Game over."

Dante let out a frustrated sigh. Damien tried to calm him down by speaking in a hushed voice. "Come on, mate. I'll show you where the heart pills are in the tent. You can help us by monitoring the cameras."

Inside the tent, Dante watched the video monitor, switching back and forth between the feed from the night-vision cameras Andy had set up in the room. He glanced at the team heart-rate monitors displayed on the board next to the mission objectives. His own heart rate returned to normal after he took the heart medicine, but Mikey's flat-line seemed to be mocking him.

"I'm still not seeing anything in the journal," Andy said over the radio. "Dante, do you see anything on the cameras?"

Dante checked the cameras. The journal was blank. The salt pile Damien had poured remained untouched. Activity measurements were low. "That's a negative," Dante finally replied.

"While activity is down, I'm going to find the cursed item and smudge it," Damien announced over the radio. "Maybe that'll encourage it to come out again."

"I think in the orphanage it's a deck of tarot cards in the headmaster's office," Andy informed his teammates. "It should be marked on the map. Dante can you check the large map on the mission board?"

"Sure," Dante replied, and turned around to face the map above the heart-rate monitors. Near the entrance on the first floor, he noticed a room marked with a black ink smudge to the right of where the lobby stood. "Hey, guys, there's a black mark on the headmaster's office. Does that mark where the cursed item is?" Instead of receiving a reply, he heard broken static. His own flashlight flickered on and off. Then he noticed the paranormal activity readings spike to the maximum level.

Spinning back around to the video monitor, Dante quickly flipped through the cameras. Damien had reached the lobby and was hiding underneath a bench. On the second floor, Andy was hiding in the wardrobe of the haunted room. Dante nervously bit his lip and looked back at the paranormal activity monitor; activity was still at the maximum level. When he turned back to the video monitor, he saw the wardrobe doors fly open. Andy was forcibly pulled from the cabinet. His body twisted before going limp and was tossed across the room.

"Fuck," Dante muttered. The noise distortion on the group radio crackled and broke. Activity dropped to nothing. He pressed the button on his radio. "Damien! Damien, are you okay?"

A slightly anxious English voice came over the radio. "Yeah, I'm all right. I managed to hide. Andy, you all right, mate?"

"He's dead," Dante said solemnly, then rubbed his eyes. Two of his friends were now gone.

Recognizing the strain in his friend's voice, Damien tried to remain positive. "Look, Dante," he said gently, "I'm going to come back out to the tent instead of going for the cursed item. We need to decide a game plan before attempting to finish the objectives."

Dante nodded. "All right. Hurry up...please."

TWO
ONI

A COUPLE MINUTES PASSED. Static suddenly crackled on the radio again. Noticing the activity reading spike again, Dante yelled into the radio, "Damien? Damien, did you make it out?"

Instead of coming through the radio, Damien's voice came from outside. "Yeah, thank God." He calmly lifted the entrance flap and walked into the tent.

"Jesus!" Dante cursed. "Why didn't you say anything on the radio?!"

"The radio turns to static when the ghost is hunting," Damien explained. He looked at the group heart-rate monitors on the mission board. Andy's heart rate was now a flatline, matching Mikey's below it. He sighed. "Well, that's unfortunate. Hate to see that."

"I wish you weren't so nonchalant about this, man," Dante grumbled. He looked back at the video monitor. "So what's the plan?"

Damien joined his friend in checking the video monitor and switched through the cameras. He paused on one camera placed in the corner of the haunted room. "Do you see this?"

"What?" Dante saw small glowing green orbs in the air on the video feed. "Oh, yeah. I thought that was just dust motes."

Damien put his face in his hands and laughed. "They're ghost orbs," he said. Pinching the bridge of his nose, he laughed again. "That's the third piece of evidence."

"Wait...what?" Dante did a double take. After quickly flipping through his manual to the evidence page, he scanned the list of possible evidence. At the very bottom was "ghost orbs" with a checkbox next to it. "No fucking way," he exclaimed. He checked off the final piece of evidence. On the "ghost type" page, only one remaining name was left in bold print: **oni**. "It's an *oni*?" Dante asked.

"It's an *oni*," Damien confirmed with a nod. He glanced at the mission board. The only two remaining mission objectives were to smudge the cursed item and banish the ghost. "So now that we figured out what the ghost type is, we've got two choices. We can either pack it up and end the mission now, or we can try to complete the remaining objectives." He turned to his friend. "Choice is yours, mate. I'm fine either way."

After checking the mission board, Dante looked at the payout for the remaining two objectives: smudge the cursed object and banish the ghost. In this game, $125 in reward money was nothing to laugh at. Grabbing the remaining crucifix from the equipment shelves, he turned to Damien and confidently smiled. "Let's get this ghost."

In the tent, Dante had sounded so confident in his decision to finish the remaining two objectives before ending the mission. Now that he and Damien had walked back into the haunted orphanage, however, he wasn't so sure about his decision. "Don't worry," Damien quietly said next to him. "We'll stick together for this."

The two friends entered the headmaster's office near the entrance of the building. "I think Andy said the cursed item on this map was a deck of tarot cards," Dante said, flashing his light around the room.

"Yeah, I'm surprised we didn't see it earlier," Damien commented. Both he and Dante had searched the office at the beginning of the mission but hadn't found anything. At the headmaster's desk, Damien searched each drawer. The only object he found was a small key; aside from the heart-shaped handle, it looked like a regular key. "Hey, Dante," he said. "Instead of a deck of cards, look for something like a safe or locked cabinet."

"Okay," Dante replied. He was on the other side of the desk, scanning through a large bookshelf that lined the office wall. One book seemed to stand out among the others. It was a large, red leather hardcover book with *The Occult* printed in gold on the spine. Dante grabbed the book and inspected it. The book made a hollow sound as if it were a box with something inside. On the cover was a clasp with a small heart-shaped lock sealing the book closed. Dante gasped. "Dude! I think I found it!"

Damien came over with the key, which slid easily into the lock. The book opened with a click, revealing a hollowed-out hiding place carved into the middle of the pages. Inside the hiding spot was a black deck of glowing cards. "Yes, this is it," Damien said quietly. He placed the open book on the desk, then got the smudge stick out of his inventory and grabbed a lighter. "As soon as I light this, the ghost is going to probably become even more pissed off," he warned his friend. "So when I drop the stick in the book, hide in the closet over there, yeah?"

Dante scanned the room to see which closet Damien was talking about. Back near the entrance of the office were two doors, one labeled Lavatory and the other Janitorial. He looked back to his friend and nodded, signaling he was ready.

"All right." Damien held his breath as he brought the lighter to the smudge stick. "Three, two, one...go!" As soon as the stick started to smoke, he dropped it into the book on top of the card deck. Dante was in front of him, moving toward the janitor's closet.

Dante opened the janitorial closet and climbed inside. Just as he was about to shut the door, Damien jumped into the cramped closet with him. "What the fuck, man?" Dante whispered. "Go find your own hiding spot!"

Damien put his hand over his mouth and let out a hushed giggle. "Relax," he replied. "We can both fit."

"I swear to God, if—" Dante's complaining was cut short when their flashlights started flickering. A nervous grimace was plastered on his face. Damien giggled again. "Shut up, shut up, shut up!" Dante whispered through gritted teeth.

"I can't help it," Damien replied, still chuckling breathlessly. "Your stupid face looks too damn funny!"

Suddenly they heard the loud thump of footsteps approaching the office. The stomping made a circle inside the room. When it sounded like the person—or entity—was about to leave, Dante sighed, exhaling loudly after holding his breath. The footsteps paused, then practically ran for the closet. The door opened and Damien was dragged out of the closet by his neck. "Shit," he exclaimed, laughing loudly. "Sorry, mate. It looks like I'm dead. Bye!"

Dante watched in horror as his last remaining friend was twisted into a pretzel and thrown behind the desk.

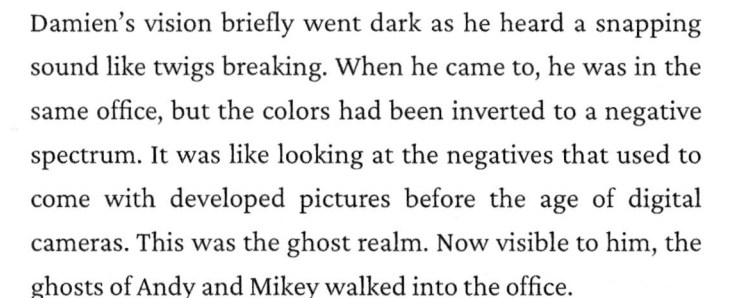

Damien's vision briefly went dark as he heard a snapping sound like twigs breaking. When he came to, he was in the same office, but the colors had been inverted to a negative spectrum. It was like looking at the negatives that used to come with developed pictures before the age of digital cameras. This was the ghost realm. Now visible to him, the ghosts of Andy and Mikey walked into the office.

"Hey, guys," Damien said with a wave.

"Hi," Mikey replied with a wave of his own. "Welcome to the afterlife."

Damien chuckled in return.

"Did you guys manage to get the third piece of evidence?" Andy asked in a more serious tone.

"Yeah, it was ghost orbs." Damien nodded. "The ghost is an *oni*." He checked his manual and saw the cursed item objective was crossed off. At least he'd managed to do that before he died.

"So what's left to do?" Mikey asked, checking his own manual. "Banish the ghost? Can Dante do that?"

"Do we even want him to try?" Andy added. "If he ends the mission now, we'll at least still get paid. If we wipe, then this was all for nothing."

All three ghosts turned and looked at Dante, who was still crouched in the closet. "What do I do?" As he was unable to hear his friends, they knew he was talking to himself. He looked at the crucifix in his hand. "Should I try banishing the ghost? Is it even my job to banish it?"

"Fuck..." Damien muttered in response. He turned to Andy and Mikey. "I'm going to have to use the ghost line to talk to him." The ghost line was a one-time-use lifeline for fallen teammates to talk to the surviving members of their group. The downside was that it cost the group $50 of their total payout and only allowed for thirty seconds of communication through the group radio.

"Do it." Andy nodded. "Dante is stupid enough to think he can banish the ghost on his own. Besides, you're supposed to use salt to banish an *oni*, not a crucifix."

"All right, here goes nothing," Damien replied.

As Dante took a step outside of the closet, the group radio crackled to life. "Hello, Dante?" Damien's voice echoed. It sounded much more hollow and distant compared to when he was alive.

"Damien?!" Dante replied in surprise. "Where are you? Are you okay?"

"I told you I was dead, mate." Damien laughed. "Look, I don't have long. I had to use the ghost line and it only gives me thirty seconds to talk to you."

Dante nodded. "Okay."

Damien's voice started to break up over the radio. "Dante, do... I repeat...try to banish the ghost. Just...we accomplished...end the mission. Banishing...requires—" Suddenly his voice was cut off.

"Hello? Hello, Damien?" Dante said into the radio.

The only reply he received was white noise. Thirty seconds offered almost no time to understand anything. Even worse, although the message was heard loud and clear in the ghost realm, Dante only heard bits and pieces of what Damien had tried to tell him.

Dante stared at the crucifix in his hand again. He believed banishing the ghost required the crucifix, but he wasn't sure what to do with it. Was he supposed to hold it out in front of him? Did he have to say anything? Or would he just have to try throwing it at the ghost if it came toward him?

Either bravely or stupidly, Dante climbed the stairs again to the second floor. "What the hell am I doing?" he muttered. "Why am I even still here?"

As if in response, a loud crash came from the haunted room. Dante jumped then froze. His eyes scanned the darkness, but he saw nothing. Taking a deep breath, he continued forward. Just as he reached the door to the haunted room, his flashlight flickered. "Fuck," he cursed, fumbling to grab the crucifix from his inventory.

At that moment, a shadowy figure appeared in the doorway. "Hey! You look nothing like a fucking *oni*," Dante yelled. Then he held the crucifix out in front of him. "Back, demon," he commanded, but the figure kept slowly walking straight toward him. For each step the ghost took toward Dante, he took a step back.

"Why isn't it working?" he questioned in a panic. Desperate, he hurled the crucifix at the *oni*. It passed harmlessly through the shadow and landed with a clank on the floor. "Oh, shit," Dante whispered breathlessly. Finally he realized he was in trouble.

He turned and ran down the hallway at the snail's pace set for his character. "This isn't working," he shrieked. Then he thought back to what Andy had told the group at the beginning of the mission: *If the ghost is on the second floor, either hide or try to lap it until you get to the stairs.* It was worth a shot.

Holding his breath, Dante ducked into one of the large

bedrooms. After racing past the creepy children's beds lining the walls, he reached what looked like a closet at the end of the room. He scrambled to open the door and crawled inside, closing the door behind him. While he was crouched, he noticed a broken porcelain toilet next to him. "No way. Is this a bathroom?" he whispered.

Suddenly loud footsteps stomped into the bedroom. Dante clenched his teeth again. "Go away," he ordered in a hushed voice. In response, the footsteps came closer until they stopped in front of the bathroom door. "No, not like this," he pleaded as the door opened. The shadow figure reached for him. "No!" Dante screamed as long black claws closed around his neck. Then everything went black and he heard the snapping of bones.

When his screen loaded again, Dante was back in the group safehouse seen at the beginning of the group co-op video game *Ghost Hunt*. In-game, all four characters approached a lit-up wall at the front of the room. On a white board was a list of the mission objectives, similar to what had been listed in the tent, with dollar totals listed for each objective. Even though almost all the objectives had being completed, the reward total at the bottom of the board was an impressive $0. Next to the amount of the reward total, written in large red letters was the message "MISSION FAILED."

THREE
HELLFIRE DANTE

DANTE ANDERSON, better known by his handle "hellfiredante," was a popular content creator on the video-sharing media site VidTV. At the age of nineteen, he'd started his gaming channel as a hobby while studying neuroscience at the University of Michigan. When his channel gained popularity, he dropped out of school and moved to Los Angeles to work on his career full-time.

Now twenty-nine years old, he was considered one of the top gamers on the platform, with nearly thirty-two million subscribers. Unfortunately, his subscriber count couldn't save him from being ridiculed by his friends. On a second monitor on his desk, Dante saw Damien, Andy, and Mikey all laughing hysterically in their video group chat. Embarrassed, he firmly planted his face in his palm.

"Dante, you screamed so loud that your mic cut out." Mikey giggled, wiping a tear away from his round, babyface cheeks. "I thought for sure you blew it out."

Michael Witt, also known as "ghost_nerd," was the host of the popular podcast *Ghost Theories*, which covered various ghost stories from around the world. He had gained eleven million subscribers on VidTV for the video version of his show. Mikey was the only one of the four who was married. His wife, Kate, had just given birth to their son six months ago. In his rare downtime, he liked to join his friends in online games and usually made appearances in their individual videos. Being a new dad, however, didn't really allow him the opportunity to make gaming videos on his own channel.

"As soon as Dante was the only one left, people started spamming my chat, saying we were screwed," Andy commented with a chuckle.

Andrew Stein was Dante's friend and old college roommate. Known as "shyandy" on VidTV, he had an admirable 750k subscriber count, but he found his niche more in live streaming while playing video games. Although he was known online for his quiet, sensitive personality, Andy seemed to have a bitter, biting sarcasm when it came to Dante. Still laughing, he pushed his curly chocolate-brown hair out of his eyes. "Pfft, you're not even supposed to use the crucifix to banish an *oni*. You need to use salt, you idiot."

"Bloody hell, Dante." Damien laughed and ran a hand through his sandy-blond hair. Better known as "dayknight," Damien Knight was a gaming content creator based out of Northwood in London; his popularity rivaled that of Dante's. His channel had barely passed twenty-eight million subscribers on VidTV last month, just as he turned twenty-eight years old. Damien wasn't shy about using a face cam in most of his videos since he had gained recognition for his handsome looks. He especially garnered attention for his bright-blue eyes, which were tearing up with laughter. "Why did you try to banish the ghost? I told you not to."

"Your voice broke up during the ghost-line message," Dante mumbled, his baritone voice muffled by his palm. One of the defining characteristics that set Dante apart from other VidTV gamers was his voice. He wouldn't admit it, but his looks didn't hurt in attracting viewers either. His tanned skin, strong jaw, dark brown eyes, and wavy black hair bleached to a burnt copper were prominently displayed via face cam in all his videos.

"Excuses, excuses," Andy commented, then sighed. "All right, boys. I need to wrap up my stream. See ya later."

Just as Andy's face dropped from their group chat, Mikey's wife showed up in the background of his video feed. "Oh, I have to go too. Kate is telling me to put the baby to bed," he informed Dante and Damien.

"Hi, Kate!" Dante and Damien waved at their cameras like excited children.

"Hi, boys." She laughed and waved. "Sorry, but I need my husband back now."

Mikey said his goodbyes and left the group chat, leaving Damien and Dante alone in the game. "So what did you think of *Ghost Hunt*?" Damien inquired with a yawn. It may have been close to 7:00 p.m. in Los Angeles, but it was nearly 3:00 a.m. in the UK. "Honestly you didn't do bad for a newb."

"Thanks." Dante sighed and rubbed his forehead. "I really like the concept. It's a lot of fun to play with friends."

Damien nodded. "Could you imagine trying to do it in real life, though?" He chuckled. "I don't think we'd do very well."

Dante's eyes lit up with excitement. "Dude, that's a great idea!"

"What is?"

"We could do a ghost-hunting show in real life." Dante smiled. After ten years on VidTV, he always tried to keep an eye out for new creative content opportunities. It helped keep his channel relevant and prevented it from getting stale. "We could go to different haunted places like the ones Mikey talks about on his podcast!"

Damien laughed with uncertainty. "Are you taking the piss, mate?" When Dante's expression remained unchanged, Damien realized his friend wasn't joking. He bit his lip. "What would we do in these haunted places? Hunt ghosts? We have no experience. We couldn't even be called amateurs."

"That's what would make it interesting," Dante said with a big grin. One of his advantages over other content creators on VidTV was that he had no shame. He was willing to look like an absolute idiot in his videos for the sake of entertainment.

"And what would you call this great ghost-hunting show?" Damien asked.

The fire in Dante's eyes was so bright it was practically burning. Once the gears in his head were turning on a project, it was hard to stop him. He motioned in a gesture similar to that of a magician. "We'll call it *Dante's Inferno*!"

One Year Later

On 20th Street in the Union Station district of downtown Denver, inside a lively brew pub, Dante and Damien celebrated over dinner by ordering another round of drinks for their friends. The duo had good reason to celebrate. They'd just wrapped shooting footage at the Stanley Hotel in Estes Park for the third episode of their popular VidTV ghost-hunting show, *Dante's Inferno*. The show was garnering major attention on social media, which also had attracted product sponsors.

Inferno's popularity was partly due to the memes people made using clips from the show, which they posted on their SMS. These posts allowed the show to reach a wider audience who didn't regularly watch VidTV. By the end of the second episode, *Dante's Inferno* had more than fifty million subscribers. The only accounts more popular were those of K-pop idol groups.

Dante's charisma, mixed with his ability to appear incredibly confident and stupid at the same time, was a huge draw for viewers. He had the uncanny gut reaction of running toward whatever scared him instead of running away. It was behavior that had mimicked his game play in horror "let's play" videos. Along with Dante, Damien co-hosted the show as the calm, sensible friend to balance the chaotic energy. The third piece to the show was Mikey in the role of lore expert. His *Ghost Theories* podcast episodes coincided with the show to advertise to even more people. Although Andy had turned down being in front of the camera, he'd offered to be one of the cameramen. His friends thought he was being helpful; in actuality, his goal for doing so was to show the world just how foolish Dante could be. That, and it gave him the opportunity to get to know Dante's girlfriend better.

Jennifer White was the second cameraman and Dante's girlfriend. When it came to hiring a cameraman for the show, Dante immediately had thought of Jen. She had a talent for recording the human expression in film and was usually the one behind the camera in Dante's non-gaming review videos on his channel. At five feet, eleven inches, Jen stood at least two inches taller than Dante. She was a self-proclaimed "typical" Southern California girl with dirty-blond hair, tan skin, a lean athletic body, and a laidback attitude. Jen and Dante had been in a serious relationship for the past five years and had been living together for the last two. In addition to working as a cameraman for Dante, Jen was a licensed massage therapist and part-time tarot card reader.

With each new episode, the group seemed to bond more, which helped create the solid show Dante originally had envisioned. Now that they'd finished shooting footage for the third episode, he was thinking about where to go next.

Jen interrupted his thoughts. "I'm running to the bathroom real quick," she said in his right ear. Dante nodded and watched her maneuver through the crowded pub.

After a moment, Andy stood up from the table. The bright red glow in his cheeks indicated he had probably reached his limit for the night. "I'll be right back. I need to take a piss," he slurred.

As he stumbled away after Jen, Damien laughed into his glass. "Yeah, I bet," he mumbled before taking a drink of his pint of pale ale. He looked over to Dante to see if his friend had noticed anything amiss. Instead, Dante appeared to be lost in his own thoughts. Amused, Damien nudged a half-asleep Mikey next to him and motioned with his chin toward their friend.

Mikey startled awake after feeling Damien's bony elbow poke him in the ribs. *I'm too old for this*, he thought, reaching for the glass of water in front of him. He wasn't used to going out to bars, especially after having a child. He adjusted his silver round-rimmed glasses, his blurry vision following the direction Damien had motioned toward. Dante sat silently chewing his lip with a focus that belonged more on a physicist on the verge of a scientific discovery rather than a VidTV content creator.

"I recognize that look," Damien said in a voice loud enough for his friends to hear him over the music. "What are you planning, Dante?"

Dante remained silent, still running through various locations in his mind. The catacombs of Paris was one option. Or they could try to stay closer to Damien's home by visiting the Tower of London. Dante immediately dismissed both locations; they felt overdone. Then it hit him, a story his mom had told him when he was a child about a haunted forest in the mountains of Gifu prefecture. It was a story that had stuck with him whenever he played Japanese horror games. "Got it!" He slammed his beer mug onto the table. Excitedly looking to his friends, he exclaimed, "We're going to Japan!"

FOUR
JAPAN

A LONG TIME AGO, deep in the forest-covered mountains of Gifu prefecture, there was a traditional Japanese inn that welcomed wanderers of all kinds. The inn was famous for its natural hot springs and was a popular stop for weary travelers going back and forth between Kyoto and Edo, now known as Tokyo. Over time, it also had become popular for another reason. The innkeeper's daughter was quickly becoming known as the most beautiful woman in the region.

One fateful November night, one guest had drunk too much sake and gotten into the hot springs. Overwhelmed by the alcohol mixed with the heat from the spring, the man felt dizzy and sank into the water. The innkeeper's daughter happened to be restocking towels on the shelves near the spring when she saw the man go under. Without a second thought, she jumped into the spring and pulled him out, saving his life.

The man soon became obsessed with his savior. He believed her saving his life was an act of fate and they were destined to be together. No matter how desperate he became, however, the daughter always managed to tactfully turn him down. Unfortunately one night the man drank too much again and became aggressive. When the daughter came to collect the sake bottles from his room, he grabbed her by the wrist and demanded a reason as to why she refused to accept him. The daughter, tired of the man's rude and forceful behavior, finally replied, "My beauty would be wasted on someone like you!"

In a fit of rage, the man grabbed a dagger from his rucksack. "Then I'll make sure no one ever considers you beautiful again," he threatened. He grabbed the woman by the neck and hacked at the corners of her mouth until it was twice the length it had been. The daughter struggled in agony and managed to grab one of the empty sake bottles tipped on its side on the floor. With strength stemming from her survival instincts, she smashed the bottle against the side of her attacker's skull. Finally she scrambled to her feet and fled the room, but the damage had been done—she was permanently disfigured.

Screaming, she ran down the main hall toward her father at the front desk of the inn. Being a suspicious person, the innkeeper mistook his daughter for a bloody, vengeful ghost. Terrified, he threw a blanket over her and dragged her body to the mountains behind the inn. There, he threw her body into a well and covered his ears so he wouldn't hear her cries.

It wasn't until morning that the innkeeper realized what he had done to his daughter. After gaining consciousness and sobering up, the drunk man confessed to disfiguring the woman. He didn't realize the innkeeper would throw her down a well. Sadly, when the innkeeper called down the well to his daughter, he heard no reply. Guilt ridden, he immediately boarded up the well and sold his inn. To repent for his mistake, he dedicated the rest of his life to caring for the Yamanaka Shinto shrine down the road from the inn.

Some say the slit-mouthed woman still wanders the forest between the boarded up well and the shrine her father later cared for. If you see a woman in a kimono with a scarf covering her mouth, you should avoid her at all costs. If she sees you, she'll coyly ask if you think she's beautiful. If you answer yes, she'll pull down her scarf to reveal her disfigured mouth and sharp, demonic teeth. "How about now?" she asks before killing her victims.

Turbulence shook Dante awake from his dream of the ghost story his mother had told him when he was a child. When he was a kid, the story of the *kuchisake onna* (the slit-mouthed woman) scared the hell out of him. Now he was on a plane to Japan to search the mountains of Gifu for her. *I must be out of my goddamn mind*, he thought, rubbing his eyes.

Sitting in the window seat next to him, Jen nudged him

with her elbow. "You got quite a bit of sleep. I'm jealous," she said with a smile. She nudged him again. "Get up. I have to pee."

With a yawn, Dante stood and let Jen out. He stretched his arms over his head and went to sit back down. As he sat back in his seat, he reached across the aisle and tapped Damien on the shoulder. "Hey, did they serve breakfast?"

"Not yet, mate," Damien replied. He removed his thick black square-framed glasses and pinched the bridge of his nose. He hated having to wear his glasses for overnight flights; it was uncomfortable compared to his contact lenses. "They should be coming around soon," he added. He pulled the menu card from the backseat pocket in front of him to see what was being offered. There was a choice of scrambled eggs with sausage and toast or a breakfast sandwich with ham, egg, and cheese. *Aren't they pretty much the same thing?*

Disappointed with the choices, Damien shook his head and turned to his friend. Before he could say anything, he paused. Dante appeared out of sorts as he looked at the meal card. That expression couldn't be in response to the shitty airline food. "Hey." Damien tapped his Dante's arm. "Sorry I didn't get to ask sooner, but how are things with Jen?"

Leave it to Damien to be perceptive enough to pick up on his emotions. Dante was hardly ever honest enough to admit to himself when he was feeling down. He pressed his lips together into a thin line and exhaled a deep breath through his nose. "She's been staying in the guest bedroom," he admitted in a low voice.

"What?" Damien couldn't believe what he'd heard. "Are you mental?"

"Probably," Dante replied reluctantly.

"Dante, you two broke up two weeks ago," Damien pointed out.

"*Three* weeks ago," Dante corrected him. He sighed and shook his head. "We've been living together for over two years. I couldn't just kick her out on the street...especially in LA." He nervously fidgeted under his friend's incredulous gaze. "It's just until she can save up enough money to find her own place."

"Are you at least charging her rent for the room?" Damien asked, cocking an eyebrow. When Dante shook his head, Damien let out a short sarcastic laugh. "Jesus," he said. "Look at Mister Big 'D' Moneybags here who can afford to let his ex-girlfriend continue to stay in his house for free."

"You know your name also starts with a big 'D,' right?" Dante chuckled. "Who's the Mister Big 'D' Moneybags here who bought his mom an estate in the English countryside?"

"She always did want to live near Oxford," Damien replied with a smile. He turned his attention to the monitor in front of him. The display showed an airplane icon slowly crawling along its route across the Pacific Ocean toward Japan. Although he wasn't exactly sure where Dante was taking them, he was thrilled to be flying into the Chubu Centrair International Airport near Nagoya. It had been a little over nine years since he'd left Japan after studying in Nagoya for a year during his time in university. Hopeful the group would be staying in the city at least one night, Damien turned to Dante. "So where exactly in Japan are we going? Are we staying in Nagoya?"

Dante nodded. "We're staying there the first night. Then we're traveling to Gifu."

"*Gifu?*" Damien asked in disbelief. He knew Gifu prefecture was just north of Nagoya. It was renowned for its various hot springs in the mountains, but that was the extent of his knowledge. "Why Gifu?"

"In the mountains northwest of Gifu City, there's supposedly the ghost of a slit-mouthed woman haunting a shrine," Dante said softly to avoid attention from the other passengers. "We're going to stay at the nearby *ryokan* and check out the shrine."

"What's a *ryokan*?" Jen asked, startling both men. She had just come back from the toilet and slapped Dante on the shoulder. "Let me back in my seat."

"It's a traditional Japanese-style inn," Dante explained as he stood up. After letting Jen back into her seat, he took his own seat and turned back to Damien. "You studied in Japan, right? What do you think?"

"The *kuchisake onna*?" Damien scratched at the scruff on his chin in thought. It was one of the urban legends he'd heard while living in Nagoya. "I guess it's worth a look. I never really went to Gifu. I think we just passed through there on our way to Kyoto or Osaka." His bright-blue eyes focused on Dante, and he asked out of curiosity, "How did you hear about this place?"

"My mom grew up in Nagahama in Shiga prefecture. It's on the other side of the mountains, where the shrine is. She said the slit-mouthed woman was a popular ghost story in the area," Dante said. Noticing the confusion on his friend's face, he elaborated. "She met my dad when he was studying at the Japan Center for Michigan Universities in Hikone near Nagahama. She was taking English classes at the same school."

"Wow, I feel like a rubbish student now," Damien complained, rubbing his forehead. "I'm not familiar with any of these places."

"It's fine." Dante dismissively waved his hand. "As long as your language skills are up to par, we should be good to go. I've been studying, but you're still the expert in our group."

"Oh, great," Damien grumbled. His Japanese was definitely rusty at best. "That's comforting. Thanks."

Dante flashed him a wide-toothed grin. "No problem, buddy!" The conversation came to an end with an announcement from the flight attendant that breakfast would now be served.

FIVE
ROAD TRIP

IT WAS late afternoon when the group arrived in Nagoya via train from the airport. From Nagoya Station, they took the subway to Sakae Station. Thankfully it was only a ten-minute walk from the subway to their hotel. Once there, they settled into their rooms for some much-needed rest.

After grabbing a few snacks at a nearby convenience store, Dante gathered everyone in his room for a meeting. There, he finally revealed to the rest of the group the ghost story his mom had told him and where they'd be traveling.

"Is that why you and Damien were talking about a *ryokan*?" Jen asked. Then, after making a sudden realization, she whined, "I was hoping we'd go shopping in Tokyo while we were here."

"Jen, we're nowhere near Tokyo," Damien pointed out. "Besides, Nagoya is, like, the third or fourth largest city in Japan. Maybe you can get some shopping done here?" He looked to Dante questioningly.

"We're just staying here tonight. We've got to check out by noon tomorrow," Dante explained. "Then it's an hour-long drive to the *ryokan* in Gifu."

"Well, I'm going to get some shopping done tonight then." Jen pouted and folded her arms. "Damien, you've got to tell me where all the brand stores are here."

"Look it up on your phone." Damien motioned to her mobile resting in her lap and shook his head. "Seriously, it's been almost ten years since I studied here while in uni. I'm sure things have changed during that time."

Andy scratched his head through his thick, curly brown hair. "If you want, I'll go with you Jen," he quietly offered. "It wouldn't be fun if you got lost alone." Jen expressed her excitement by bouncing up and down on the bed.

"Well, just make sure to meet back here by nine p.m.," Dante said with a dead serious expression.

"Why?" Mikey asked warily. Was there another type of ghost that was going to haunt them after 9:00 p.m.? Would they become cursed and turn into pumpkins?

"So we can go do karaoke, of course." Dante laughed.

"Karaoke!" the group cheered in unison.

In the middle of the night, on a quiet mountain road, a heavy fog blanketed the ground. A thick green forest lined both sides of the road—one climbing farther up the mountain, the other steeply sloping downward. Damien walked alongside the road with only the crunch of his footsteps on the gravel to accompany him. The fog obscured whatever moonlight may have normally illuminated the path, leaving the intermittent streetlamps as the only source of light.

Damien hugged his arms around himself, trying to hold in whatever remaining heat he had in his body. He walked through the cold November air dressed in only a gray T-shirt and jeans. His worn black Chuck Taylors kicked at a few pebbles among the gravel. *Why didn't I bring a coat?* he wondered. The cold, damp air sent chills down his spine, and the eerie silence from the moss-covered forest next to him did nothing to help alleviate the constant shivering in his bones.

"This is bollocks," he muttered. He felt as if he'd been walking for miles, but none of the scenery had changed. Looking ahead of him, he saw the same thick fog, eerie green forest, and intermittent streetlights he'd seen when he'd looked behind him. Was he making any progress? Where was he even going?

Suddenly a streetlight flickered on with a buzz, and the fog cleared to his left. A stone torii gate and steep cobblestone staircase became illuminated in the dull yellow light. Dark-green moss claimed everything, including the stairs and gate. Damien squinted and managed to make out the kanji symbols on the gate's stone pillars. "Yama...naka?" he said quietly. He was immediately met with the disembodied giggle of a young woman. He spun around, searching the dark forest. "Hello," he called out. "Is anyone there?"

"Damien," the voice whispered in his right ear. He spun around again but found no one. The voice then whispered in his left ear, "*Matteiru ne*." Damien easily translated the informal Japanese to English in his head: *I'm waiting.* But who was waiting for him? He turned just in time to catch a glimpse of several white fox tails disappear into the fog as a shadowy figure climbed the stairs. *A kitsune?!*

Damien was pulled from his dream by a hand shaking his shoulder. "Fuck, it's bright," he mumbled, shielding his eyes from the midday sun. The dream had left him feeling disturbed. It had been years since he'd had a nightmare. The group was traveling in a minivan on their way to the Yamanaka Inn. Cursing again, Damien readjusted his black sunglasses and looked out the window to see a mix of fields and mountains in the distance. "Where the fuck are we?" he asked, yawning.

"Right outside a town called Ono in Gifu prefecture," Mikey replied from the seat next to him.

The two had claimed the seats in the back of the van when the hired driver had picked them up in Nagoya earlier that afternoon. Jen and Andy took the two middle seats and were chatting quietly. Their muted conversation was occasionally interrupted by Jen's flirtatious laughter. Dante seemed oblivious to his ex-girlfriend's behavior. He was up in the front next to the driver, excitedly asking about the *ryokan* they were heading to. The old man seemed amused by his enthusiasm.

"I don't know why I asked," Damien mumbled, rubbing his forehead. The hangover resulting from last night's karaoke excursion combined with the strange nightmare had left him in a bad mood. "I've still got no clue where we are."

"I guess it's the last town before we head up into the mountains," Mikey said, repeating what Dante had told them earlier. He was already regretting waking Damien up from his nap. "We're going to stop at the next convenience store we come across to pick up some snacks since the *ryokan* doesn't have any stores nearby."

"Jesus Christ, this place really is in the *inaka*, huh?" Damien commented. He made a mental note to pick up a few vitamin energy drinks and some squid jerky to help with his hangover.

"What does '*inaka*' mean?" Mikey asked.

"The countryside," Damien replied. "More specifically, the middle of nowhere." He pouted and scratched his chin. Maybe it was the lingering fear and ominous feeling from his creepy dream, but he couldn't help being grumpy. "Sorry for being such a knob, Mikey," he said. "I'm hanging and the jet lag doesn't help."

"No problem. I know what you mean," Mikey replied. He had become bored with the drive as soon as the group was out of Nagoya. Exhaustion was definitely setting in. Hopefully he'd get a nap in at the *ryokan* before Dante dragged them off to who knows where.

The Yamanaka Inn was at least another twenty-minute drive from Ono. The road that led up to the *ryokan* was long and wound around Mother Nature's natural obstructions. Dante noticed mirrors posted on poles where the road became a narrow blind curve. Soon he found out the purpose of the mirrors when the driver pulled over just in time for a semi-truck to fly by them going in the opposite direction down the mountain road.

"Jesus," Dante muttered. He was suddenly extremely thankful for his mom's advice to hire a driver rather than the group driving themselves. Not only did people drive on the left side of the road in Japan, but there also were extremely narrow roads where experienced drivers knew to pull off the road to let other traffic by. These areas were dangerous for the average ignorant tourist.

"Did you see? It's a monkey," the driver said, interrupting Dante's thoughts. He pointed out the passenger-side window before pulling back onto the road. "You must be lucky," the man commented. "Monkeys are good luck, you know?"

"I didn't see it," Dante replied. His eyes followed the direction where the driver was pointing, but all he saw was the deep green forest. *Are monkeys really that common in Japan?* He craned his neck to see if it was hiding among the leaves. Unfortunately he couldn't spot the creature before the driver got back onto the road.

The rest of the drive continued with silence between

Dante and the driver. Within minutes, the van turned around a winding curve before pulling into a gravel parking lot in front of a large traditional-style wooden building. "We have arrived," the driver said with smile and got out to unload the luggage from the back of the van.

"Hey, guys. We're here," Dante announced over his shoulder. His friends all seemed tired, but he was wide-awake with an excitement that ran through his body like an electric current. He jumped out of the van with the enthusiasm of a teenager and jogged to the back of the vehicle to help the driver unload the luggage. He couldn't wait to check out the well behind the *ryokan* where the innkeeper supposedly had dropped his daughter to her death.

The rest of the group slowly filed out of the van, taking time to stretch their legs. Dante already was walking into the building with his suitcase as Jen and Andy headed to the back of the van to grab their luggage.

"Does he always have to be so damn energetic?" Jen mumbled.

"Of course." Andy chuckled. "You know what he's like." He threw his duffel bag over his shoulder and noticed Jen's large suitcase. Although it had wheels on the bottom, it would be difficult to maneuver across the gravel parking lot. Before she could grab the suitcase, Andy easily picked it up by the side handle. "Got you, babe," he said quietly and winked at her.

Jen blushed furiously and smacked him on the shoulder. "Shh! Someone will hear you," she whispered.

Mikey and Damien came around to the back of the vehicle. "You guys all right?" Damien asked. Flustered, Jen only nodded and pushed Andy from behind, directing him toward the building.

"Do you think something is going on with those two?" Mikey quietly asked. He leaned down and grabbed his suitcase. "They've been pretty close lately."

Damien wasn't amused as he watched the two enter the building. He'd also noticed the increasingly flirtatious behavior between Jen and Andy. Was Dante that ignorant about his ex, or was he actually okay with how close the two were? "I don't know," Damien finally replied. He grabbed his suitcase by the top handle and let out a sigh. "It's not really any of our business."

Mikey nodded. "Good point," he said softly.

After unloading the last of the luggage, the driver quickly shut the doors and got back in the van. Confused, Damien knocked on the driver's-side window. The driver rolled down the window just enough to speak to them. "Eh?" he asked.

"Where you off to?" Damien asked. Was the driver going to abandon them in the mountains? "Aren't you staying here?"

The old man chuckled. "Nah, I don't stay here. I'll be staying with a friend in town," he explained. What he didn't say was there was no way in hell he would stay in these cursed woods. He didn't even know how Mr. Yamada, the inn's owner, managed to live here. "See you in two days," he said with a smile and rolled up the window.

Before Damien could protest, the man peeled out of the

gravel parking lot with a squeal and took off back down the mountain toward Ono. *What the hell was that?* Damien wondered.

"He's not staying here?" Jen yelled to Damien from the entrance to the *ryokan*. Damien shook his head. She looked to Andy with concern. "What if we have an emergency or something?"

Andy shrugged. "The innkeeper probably has a vehicle." He motioned with his chin to a large wooden shed that resembled a barn. "Maybe it's in there."

Jen sighed. No transportation left her feeling uneasy. Damien and Mike joined them at the entrance, and the four friends made their way into the *ryokan*. "I don't like this one bit," Jen mumbled.

SIX
YAMANAKA INN

THE ENTRANCE to the inn was a large room separate from the main lobby. Several wooden shelves with lockers lined the room. Damien immediately recognized the *genkan*, an elevated wooden floor that was a step up from the stone-tiled entranceway to the rest of the building. "Hold up, guys. We have to take off our shoes," he informed the group as he untied his black Chuck Taylors. After choosing a random open locker, he put his shoes in and grabbed the large wooden key. Mikey, Andy, and Jen followed his lead and placed their shoes in lockers as well.

Before heading into the lobby, Damien noticed two shelves with green vinyl guest slippers. He grabbed a pair for himself and slipped them on before grabbing a pair for each of his friends. As he heard Dante's boisterous laughter from inside the lobby, he hoped his friend was knowledgeable enough to have removed his shoes.

The lobby was barely larger than the entrance area. The check-in counter took up most of the room as it expanded from the left wall and wrapped in an *L* shape. On the right side of the room, there was just enough space for two cushioned chairs and a small end table between them. Shoji screen doors and ornate wood carvings above the doors made up the entire back wall.

Damien looked around the room and decided it was better described as "cozy" instead of "small." He joined Dante at the counter, where his friend was talking with the innkeeper. With a small sigh of relief, he noticed Dante was wearing guest slippers.

"*Sumimasen ga,*" Damien spoke in his rusty Japanese.

"Hey, hey, hey." The innkeeper stopped him by holding up his right hand. He appeared to be in his early to mid-forties with straight chocolate-brown hair, black eyes, and a permanent exhausted expression. The man took business casual to the extreme, wearing a navy blue zip-up sweatshirt, a plain white T-shirt underneath, and black Adidas track pants. "I used to be an English teacher. You can speak English," he said in a deep, raspy voice. He pulled out a pack of cigarettes from the right pocket of his hooded sweatshirt. After taking one out of the pack, he placed it between his lips. "Kazuya Yamada," he mumbled his introduction as he lit his cigarette.

"D-damien Knight," Damien returned the introduction and coughed. He found it odd that Mr. Yamada had such a blatant disregard for his guests. Maybe smoking was still widely acceptable in the Japanese countryside. Still, he couldn't overlook the innkeeper's bad habit, especially when he had asthma. To relay his discomfort, he coughed again while looking Mr. Yamada in the eyes.

Mr. Yamada stared directly back at him to express how much he didn't care. After a moment, he rolled his eyes and opened the shoji screen door behind him to ventilate the room. The screen slid back to reveal an outdoor traditional Japanese rock garden complete with lanterns and a canopy of bare cherry trees. Moss covered the stone lanterns that lined the area. The garden was probably beautiful in the spring when the cherry blossoms bloomed. With it being November and the trees being bare, however, it resembled a cemetery more than a garden.

On the other side of the garden, Dante noticed a path that led up into the forest. As Mr. Yamada continued to check in his guests, Dante nudged Damien and motioned toward the path. Damien craned his neck to see what his friend was so excited about, saw the path, and shook his head. He was too exhausted for this.

"Mr. Yamada," Dante started to say.

"Call me Kaz," the innkeeper interrupted him.

"Um...okay, Kaz," Dante replied. Barely containing his excitement, he continued, "Is it true there's a well in the woods behind the *ryokan*?"

Kaz gave him a tired look, as if nosy tourists had asked him this question hundreds of times. He took a deep drag and exhaled. The hazy smoke lingered in the air before slowly dissipating. "Are you here to find the *kuchisake onna*?" he asked in a low tone.

Dante's eyes lit up. "Yes, we are. Do you know where we can find her?"

Kaz's indifference couldn't be more evident. He took another drag on his cigarette. Pointing to the path, he gave his usual spiel to ghost-hunting foreigners. "Take the path up into the mountain forest and you'll come across a boarded-up well. That's supposedly where the father threw his daughter to her death. Please don't touch the well or attempt to remove the cover. The other site is the Yamanaka Shinto Shrine just down the road." He slowly blinked and added, "I wouldn't go out at night, though."

By now the whole group was listening intently. "Pfft." Andy broke the silence and folded his arms in a weak, masculine attempt to appear unafraid. "Why not?" he challenged their host. "Dude, I'm not scared."

Taking a deep breath, Kaz leaned on the counter with his right hand and glared at Andy with a menacing look. He loudly exhaled, blowing smoke out through his nostrils. The haze rose, partially obscuring his stern face. Andy flinched as the man's black eyes appeared to flash red from behind the smoke. "You never know what you'll find in a mountain forest at night," he finally replied in a dark tone.

Before anyone could register their fear of their host, he blinked and was back to the same energy of an overworked, middle-aged, businessman. "That reminds me," he mumbled, his cigarette still in his mouth. He ducked underneath the counter and produced a yellow laminated pamphlet. "This is the menu for tonight's dinner." Pointing at one item toward the top of the menu, he continued, "There is a side of red miso soup with wild boar meat."

"Great," Jen commented from behind the boys. Her vegetarian stomach lurched at the thought of eating boar for dinner. Her uneasiness was quickly building into fatigue and nausea.

After Kaz showed the group to their room, they exchanged glances. The room had traditional tatami mat floors and a large closet with sliding doors lining one of the walls. Inside the closet was a set of futons to sleep on. The group was lucky to have a private toilet attached to their room, although there was no shower. Guests were expected to bathe in the hot springs. The room was considered barren by Western standards but was expected for a *ryokan*.

"Oh, no way!" Damien exclaimed, racing to one side of the room where there was a short coffee table with a quilted rug underneath. A thick blanket was coming out from just beneath the tabletop surface. In the center of the table was a bowl of tangerines.

Dante watched his friend turn on a small switch and get under the blanket. "What is that?" he asked. Then a memory came back to him from when he was ten years old and his mom had taken him to visit family in Japan over the New Year's holiday. "A *kotatsu*?!" he gasped and jumped under the blanket spreading out from the table.

"This is one of the things I missed the most after leaving Japan." Damien laughed as he grabbed one of the tangerines and peeled it. Suddenly he noticed the confusion on his friends' faces.

Dante grabbed a tangerine and peeled it too. "Come have a seat, guys." He motioned for them to come to the table. "There's a heater underneath here," he said with a smile.

Mikey gladly put his luggage down and climbed under the blanket. He had read that Japanese homes, especially traditional ones, didn't usually have central heating and cooling. Sure enough, he noticed a small air conditioner unit hanging high up on the wall in the corner of the room. Grabbing a tangerine, he moved over to allow room for Jen and Andy to get under the thick blanket. "So what's the plan, boss?" he asked Dante.

Finished peeling his tangerine, Dante broke the fruit apart and popped a piece into his mouth. Checking the time on his phone, he saw it was just past 4:00 p.m. "It's going to be dark soon, so we should save the shrine for tomorrow," he thought out loud. "We'll head up there during the day to film some footage and figure out where everything is. It'll be difficult to navigate the woods in the dark without seeing it in the daylight first."

"But the innkeeper warned us we shouldn't go up there in the dark," Andy said. He gave Jen a worried glance, expecting her to say something to rein in her ex-boyfriend. Jen appeared to have absolutely no energy, though. In fact, she looked like she was about to pass out.

"Kaz doesn't need to know," Dante said in a low voice. "We'll sneak out tomorrow night and walk up to the shrine ourselves." He had a manic gleam in his eyes. "For now, let's head out to the well before it gets dark."

"I'm going to stay here," Jen interjected. Her left elbow was propped up on the table with her head resting in her hand. "I've had a weird feeling since we got here. Maybe I just need some rest."

"I'll stay with her," Andy offered, looking from Jen to Dante. "Someone should stay with her." Only Mikey could see Andy place a hand on Jen's lower back. He closed his eyes and tried to ignore it. Like Damien had said earlier, it was none of his business.

Dante wasn't good at hiding his disappointment. "But if both of you stay here, how are we supposed to get footage of the well?" he said, annoyed. Sure, Mikey usually carried a small handheld camera on their excursions, but Andy and Jen were the actual cameramen. They were experienced with filming the show on professional cameras. Although they were never in the series itself, the show wouldn't exist without them.

Not wanting an argument to ensue, Mikey raised his hand. "Maybe the footage of the well would look better on the handheld camera, at least for now," he said. "Maybe it'll make it reminiscent of *The Ring* or found-footage analog horror. Then, when Jen's feeling better, we can get some more professional footage of it."

"He does have a point," Damien said. He looked to Dante and cocked an eyebrow. "What do you think?"

Dante closed his eyes and let out a deep sigh. "Fine," he conceded. "Damien, Mikey, and I will go look for the well before the sun sets." He pointed to Jen and Andy with his index and middle fingers. "You two get some rest. You'll need it for tomorrow."

SEVEN
ON

BEHIND THE *RYOKAN*, Dante, Damien, and Mikey started their short hike up the mountain path in search of the well from the ghost story. Mikey had his handheld camera running as the other two men walked in front of him. As Dante looked back at him, Mikey nodded to signal he was ready to start filming.

"Hello there! Hellfiredante here, back with another ghost-hunting video," Dante turned around to face the camera and walked backward while delivering his opening for *Dante's Inferno*. "Today we're in the mountains of Japan in search of the slit-mouthed woman," he said with animated hand gestures. "I'm here with my good friends Damien and Mikey, otherwise known as dayknight and ghost_nerd. Say hello, fellas."

"Hello, fellas," Damien cheekily replied, waving at the camera.

Mikey then turned the camera on himself. "Hello," he

said with a chuckle, then turned the camera back on Dante and Damien.

As Dante went into a short summary of the ghost story, Damien marveled at his quick ability to turn on his video persona. For Dante, it was like flicking on a light switch. Hellfiredante was a persona that had his own characteristics but amplified by ten. Whereas Dante was self-assured and confident, hellfiredante was overly confident, conceited, and had an ego the size of California. His bigheaded character was how he was able to build up over thirty-two million subscribers to his VidTV channel. Why mess with a winning formula?

Damien had difficulty keeping on top of his schedule whenever he was struggling to be "on" for his videos. He'd been known to take mental health breaks that sometimes lasted months. Thankfully he had a great fanbase that was understanding and didn't abandon his channel. That still didn't ease the guilt he felt whenever he returned from a long break.

"So Dante..." Damien looked to his friend as they climbed up the path. "Where are we heading?" It was a setup for Dante to explain to the viewers, of course.

"I'm so glad you asked," Dante said with a smile and faced the camera again. "Right now we're looking for the well tha—" A loud thud suddenly came from the woods, cutting off Dante's speech and causing the men to jump.

"What the fuck was that?" Damien whispered.

"It could have been an old log," Dante whispered back. The three men scanned the woods around them but didn't see anything. "Should we keep going?" he asked in a hushed voice. He then turned to the camera and gave it a wink. "I think we should keep going."

Back at the *ryokan*, Jen pulled out one of the futons from the closet and set it up so she could lie down. Andy helped by grabbing a blanket and pillow for her. Once her futon was set up, Jen lay down and sighed.

"Hey, are you going to be okay?" Andy asked, pulling out a futon for himself and spreading it out next to hers. After grabbing a blanket and pillow, he slid the closet door shut. "Are you really not feeling well?"

"Yes, I'm really not feeling well," Jen retorted in a snarky tone. Taking a moment to check her attitude, she groaned with frustration. "Sorry. It's this place. I don't like it. I can't describe it." She looked up at him. "It gives me this icky feeling, like something bad is going to happen."

"I'm sorry," Andy said, pointlessly. It wasn't within his power to control the environment. Still, he did feel sorry. Looking at his interlaced fingers, he mumbled, "I thought maybe you wanted to stay behind to get away from Dante and be alone with me."

With a tired expression, Jen blinked at him and exhaled. "Are you really going to do this right now?"

"Well, what the fuck, Jen?" Andy defended himself. "A month ago you told me you were going to break up with that idiot, but you're still living with him!" He took a deep breath and sighed. "I don't like my girlfriend living with her ex."

Jen rubbed her forehead in frustration. "Who said I wanted another boyfriend right away?"

Andy may have been the one to confess his feelings in Denver and encourage her to break up with Dante, but she wasn't fully committed to the thought of jumping into yet another serious relationship. Honestly she felt being single might be a good opportunity to do some soul-searching. This wasn't the time to discuss her thoughts with Andy, though. Her splitting headache cleaved a path through her frontal lobe, not allowing many thoughts at all. She sighed and reached out her right hand to lightly touch Andy's fingers. "Just wait until this trip is over, okay? I'll try to find my own place by then."

Andy nodded, setting aside his insecurities, and leaned over to kiss her forehead. "Get some rest, Sleeping Beauty," he said softly.

Jen responded with a smile and closed her eyes. It wasn't that she didn't like being with Dante. He always made her laugh, and he was generally kind to everyone. Her issue with him was that he always placed his career first and didn't seem to care about her. They had been together for over five years, but Dante always seemed to change the subject when she brought up marriage. She had met Andy through Dante when they'd started dating. Jen and Andy had bonded over their common interest in filming and soon became friends after that.

It wasn't until they were in Colorado when she finally

noticed Andy seemed to care for her more than Dante did. At the brew pub in Denver, Andy had pulled her outside for a moment to confess his feelings to her. Jen was surprised, but she knew she felt the same. She promised to break up with Dante so she and Andy could be public about their relationship, but both fear and lack of income had delayed her search for her own place to live. As she drifted off to sleep, one question kept running through her head: *How will Dante react?*

In the forest, the three men continued up the path but now at a slower pace. Their walk was accompanied with an eerie silence and an occasional few chirps. Eventually the path opened up to a clearing; in the center was a simple stone well. Behind the well stood a wall of solid mountain rock that led up to a cliff about fifteen feet high. Dante made a shocked expression, his mouth forming an *O* as he slowly turned toward the camera. "I think we're here," he whispered.

Damien didn't like the area. He shivered and looked around. Aside from the cliff face, the clearing was surrounded by a thick green forest, which left him feeling claustrophobic. "Hey, Dante," he said softly. "Let's get out of here. I don't like this."

Dante, still in character, replied with a "Pffft!" then laughed. "What are you afraid of? Do you think the *kuchisake onna* is coming to get us?" Playfully he slapped his friend's arm and continued toward the well. "It'll be fine," he said confidently.

"Mate, this isn't a bit—I'm dead serious." Damien stared at his friend. Suddenly another loud thud resounded in the distance, along with what sounded like wooden blocks tapping together. "Jesus Christ!" Damien responded with a flinch. His blue eyes searched the forest in the direction the sound had come from. "Dante! Over there," he shouted and pointed.

"What is it?" Dante followed the direction Damien was pointing. In the distance, a shadowy figure appeared to be watching them. His heart pounded with adrenaline, and his eyes lit up with excitement. "Gah!" he yelled, running toward the figure. It was his battle cry, his signature move. He refused to ever run away from anything, no matter how frightened he was.

Mikey kept his camera trained on Dante until he disappeared into the brush. Feeling an icy shiver up his spine, Mikey ran over to Damien. "What the hell was that?" he asked quietly.

"I have no idea," Damien replied and shook his head. This was the fourth episode of *Dante's Inferno* they were filming, and this was the first time Damien actually had seen something. A genuine fear crept into his bones, causing the hair on the back of his neck to stand on end.

Always in search of lore, Mikey turned his camera toward the well and zoomed in to see what he could find. The well itself looked securely boarded up. In front was a moss-covered plaque. "Hey, Damien. Do you know what this says?" he asked, walking toward the plaque.

Damien turned to see the plaque in front of the well. He walked closer until he was next to Mikey. Moss obscured most of the lettering, but Damien could make out bits of it. "Looks like a memorial," he said. He squinted and focused on the *kanji* symbol for "child." "I think this might be her name. It looks like her family name was Hikari, but her first name is covered by moss. It ends with *–ko*, which is pretty common for Japanese girl names." He touched the character on the plaque. "I wonder what her first name was," he mumbled, almost as if in a trance.

Hearing a rustle from the woods behind them, both men spun around. Dante emerged from the forest unharmed but out of breath. He had a long stick hoisted over his right shoulder. "I couldn't find anything," he said with a big smile and nodded at the camera. "If there *was* a ghost, I guess hellfiredante was too much for it."

"Whatever." Damien sighed. "Can we leave now?"

"No way!" Dante replied. "I want to see the well too."

"It's nothing remarkable," Mikey said. "Just a boarded-up well and a moss-covered plaque." Aside from the creepy shadow in the woods, he thought the area was pretty dull in relation to the ghost story. Or perhaps it was his own self-preservation instincts that made him want to get out of there. "Let's head back, man."

"Fine, fine," Dante conceded with a wave of his hand. Dramatically picking up his stick and swinging it until it pointed to the path they had taken to the clearing, he exclaimed, "Back to the inn!"

The three men walked across the clearing to the path and started their short hike down to the *ryokan*. Mikey looked back to the area one last time before it became obscured by trees. Turning off his camera, he ran to catch up with Dante and Damien. "Dante, was there really nothing in the woods?" he asked, panting from his jog.

"Yeah, nothing was out there," Dante replied in his normal voice. The long stick now became a makeshift walking stick. "I thought I saw a figure, but when I reached the spot, it disappeared." He kicked a stone off the path. "It was weird."

"That place seriously creeped me out," Damien mumbled, and shivered. As he hugged his arms around his body, he remembered his dream from earlier. He tried to shake the nightmare from his mind and told himself to stay logical. "Maybe the figure was just some shadows from the sun going down."

"Maybe," Dante agreed, then turned to Mikey. "Were you able to catch all the strange stuff on camera?" he asked with hope in his voice. The area itself felt like a letdown, but some content was better than nothing.

"Yeah, I think so." Mikey exhaled. "I kept recording even when you ran into the woods." Although the hike down the path wasn't strenuous, he felt short of breath. The precipitation in the air felt like it was bearing down on his chest. "This place gives me the creeps too," he said quietly. "The air feels really heavy."

Dante nodded. "Kaz told me fog is pretty common up here. On the plus side, we can put the well out of our minds for the rest of the night." He switched to a chipper tone. "I don't know about you guys, but I can't wait to soak in the hot springs." Mikey and Damien perked up as the three discussed Japanese bathing culture and hot springs. It was a welcome distraction from their eerie experience moments ago.

EIGHT
DÉJÀ VU

THE NEXT MORNING, Dante's eyes opened at the first purple and pink slivers of light from the crack of dawn. He looked around the tatami room to find all his friends sleeping peacefully on their futons. He tiptoed around the bodies as if they were graves. *What an odd thought.* He then went to the bathroom to brush his teeth and change into some sweats. Coming out of the bathroom, he noticed Jen was awake. "Hey, I'm going for a run," he whispered to her.

"Okay. I'm going back to sleep." She rolled over, throwing the covers over her head.

After walking through the gravel parking lot, Dante ran down the mountain road toward where the shrine was located. The image of his ex-girlfriend's troubled face was stuck in his mind. It bothered him; Jen hadn't been her usual relaxed self since they'd arrived at the inn. When Dante had returned with Damien and Mikey late yesterday afternoon, she was sleeping and continued to sleep until

9:00 p.m. She only got up to take a bath in the hot springs and returned to her futon afterward. She didn't even touch her dinner, claiming she wasn't hungry.

In fact, Jen wasn't the only one acting strange since their arrival at the Yamanaka Inn. Damien complained of having chills all night, even though he didn't have a fever. Andy was even more cantankerous than usual, snapping at Dante during dinner for venturing out into the woods by himself. Finally, Mikey could be heard throwing up in the middle of the night. Dante was the only one who seemed to be in good spirits. *Maybe I should take them to Tokyo after this is over.*

"Whoa!" Dante was so preoccupied that he nearly missed the entrance to the shrine. Just as he saw the stone torii gate, he tried to slow down on the gravel beside the road and rolled his right ankle in the process. "Fuck!" he exclaimed. He tried walking on it; although it hurt like hell, it didn't feel sprained. "Well, looks like I won't be continuing my run," he huffed, placing his hands on his hips. He took a moment to examine the entrance to the shrine as he paced on the side of the road.

The sun was starting to rise, revealing a thick carpet of moss covering the gate and stairs, similar to the rock garden behind the inn. Kanji symbols were carved into the stone pillars. Even with the obstructive moss, Dante made out the simple kanji for "mountain" and "middle" on the stone sign. *Yamanaka.* These were the same symbols that were on the inn. This confirmed he had the right place. "I'll see you in a bit." He pointed to the gate and began his painful walk back up to the *ryokan*. *Looks like I'm going to need that stick from yesterday.*

It was after 11:00 a.m. by the time the group finished breakfast, gathered their equipment, and made their way toward the shrine. Although Dante was certain he hadn't sprained his ankle, Jen insisted on wrapping it in a bandage. Whether it was the bandage or the injury, he walked with a bit of a limp. Thankfully the shrine wasn't far from the inn, and he had his handy walking stick to help him.

As the group made their way to the shrine, Mikey took out his camera to film the intro for the corresponding episode of his podcast. "What's up, guys! Avid ghost_nerd Mikey here, back with another episode of..." He paused for dramatic effect then growled, "*Ghost Theories*!" He turned his camera to take a wide shot of the forest beside the road and continued his narration. "We're here with Dante and Damien on day two of our ghost hunt in Japan!"

"Day three," Andy rudely interrupted Mikey's opening monologue. Everyone turned to glare at him with confusion. From the very beginning of the show, Andy had never expressed interest in being on camera. "What?" he snapped back at the group. "It's our third day in Japan."

"Yeah, but day two since we've been filming, mate," Damien corrected him.

Andy rolled his eyes in response but thankfully kept his

mouth shut. Arguing would have just continued to make everyone miserable.

"Thanks, Damien," Mikey said quietly before turning the camera back on himself. "Hey, editor, take that part out, please," he noted, then took a deep breath and continued his monologue.

Much like Dante's video persona, the ghost_nerd was an over-the-top version of Mikey. Whereas he had an interest in ghost stories and lore, the ghost_nerd version of himself discussed those stories with an extremely animated voice. His wife, Kate, often gently teased him for being a geek. At the same time, she was an avid supporter of his hobby-turned-career.

With a master's degree in journalism and media from the University of Texas at Austin, Mikey firmly believed he was meant to be an investigative reporter in some form. Although his podcast had reached a million subscribers by the time he had met Dante and Damien at a content creator convention in New York City five years ago, he saw his subscriber number leap higher after he started regularly appearing in his friends' videos. Unlike Andy, Mikey was never jealous of the popularity Dante and Damien had on VidTV. He felt his dynamic voice was much more entertaining in a podcast than if he appeared in front of the camera with his "dad bod" and round baby face.

Fidgeting with his glasses, Mikey wrapped up his monologue and aimed his camera toward Dante's back. "Are we there yet?" he jokingly whined like a toddler.

"Actually this is it!" Dante exclaimed as the group

approached the stone gate. Jen and Andy took that as their cue to turn on their cameras and began filming. Dante turned to them in full hellfiredante character. "This"—he motioned with his right arm to the gate—"is the entrance to the Yamanaka Shinto Shrine. Many centuries ago, the innkeeper supposedly spent the rest of his life caring for the shrine as a way of repenting for killing his daughter. In these very woods is where the *kuchisake onna* is said to appear." He spoke in a hushed voice. "Should we check it out?"

As Dante flirted with the camera and his future viewers, Damien scanned their surroundings. He had seen several shrines during his time studying in Nagoya, so seeing the stone torii should have felt familiar and welcoming. It was familiar, but it was more in the sense of déjà vu. Suddenly a chill ran over his arms. His eyes opened wide, and he looked to his right to see an old wooden streetlight. It was daylight, but everything was identical to what he'd seen in his creepy dream.

"Wh-what?" Damien managed to whisper.

It felt like his throat was closing, and his breaths came quicker. It had been well over six months since his last panic attack. He hadn't even considered packing his anti-anxiety meds. He hugged his arms around himself and stared at the ground. As he looked down, he noticed he was wearing blue jeans, black Chuck Taylors, and a gray T-shirt, just like in his dream. The only difference was the navy-blue fleece-lined hooded jacket over his T-shirt. "Fuck," he muttered. "I can't breathe."

"Damien, are you okay?" Jen noticed her friend acting strange. He turned back to look at her with desperation in his eyes, and she saw he was struggling to breathe. "Damien!" she yelled as she ran over to him and managed to catch him before he could collapse. "Someone help me move him," she ordered, looking to the rest of the group.

Mikey came forward to help her usher Damien to sit down on the stone stairs. Sitting next to her friend on the steps, Jen rhythmically patted his back and counted out deep breathing exercises. It was a tactic she'd learned while taking care of her autistic younger brother whenever he had a meltdown.

Dante could only look on, frozen and helpless. He never was one to keep a level head during emergencies. Thankfully Damien appeared to be calming down, thanks to Jen. Dante finally asked his friend, "Are you okay to keep going or do you want to head back?"

"Dante, how could you ask him that?! Don't you see how upset he is?" Jen scolded him.

"It's okay," Damien softly told her, then looked up to Dante. "I'm fine. This place just weirded me out is all."

"Okay then." Dante took a deep breath and helped Damien to his feet.

The group pressed on and climbed the stairs together. Dante led the way, with Damien and Mikey following close behind. Being the cameramen, Jen and Andy brought up the rear.

Farther up the stairs, their environment took on a deep-green hue. Moss continued to claim everything in the forest, causing some steps to be uneven and slippery. Jen spent most of her time looking at the ground so she could safely navigate the climb in her wedge-heeled boots. The boots were cute for fall but far from ideal for being in the outdoors. She took a shaky step onto a small platform where the stairs turned in a different direction to climb farther up the mountainside.

Just as Jen looked up from the ground, her face smacked into some low-hanging tree branches. The thin twigs whipped at her cheeks like a cat-o'-nine tails, then tangled in her dirty-blond hair. "Ow!" she screamed, and tried to untangle herself from the limbs. It felt as if the tree had grabbed her by the hair and was pulling her backward. "Help!" she cried to the guys.

Dante spun around and was about to go to her aid. Andy stopped him by holding up a hand. "I'll do it," he said. Calmly he descended the stairs and helped Jen detangle her hair from the dead-looking branches. "You okay?" he asked softly as he smoothed down her hair.

"Yeah, I think so," she said, breathless from screaming. Her eyes darted back to the tree and she glared at it with anger. She considered if she should break off a branch in retaliation. *No, it's just a tree*, she reminded herself.

"Here. Go ahead of me." Andy waved his arm ahead of him. "We don't want any more trees kidnapping you," he joked.

Jen let out small laugh. "Thanks." She continued the climb until she caught up behind Mikey. "Okay, I'm all right," she said, sighing.

The group continued their climb, going through various stone torii gates resembling the one at the road entrance. The ground beneath the trees appeared to slope steeply down the mountain. In the distance was the sound of a stream, but otherwise it was unnervingly quiet.

Finally they passed through one last gate on the stairs and reached a large, flat, open area with a stone path going directly down the middle. On the right side of the path was a guardian lion dog statue with its mouth open. On the left side was a similar statue with its mouth closed. Not even the statues were immune to the moss, which seemed to grow everywhere.

The friends continued down the path through another stone torii gate to an open stone tiled area that resembled a courtyard. Various buildings lined the square. On the left were structures that looked like abandoned festival stalls. At the far end of the square stood the main shrine, blocked off with a huge thick rope and paper hanging down. The building to the right resembled a smaller version of the *ryokan* where they were staying. Unlike the *ryokan*, however, this building had a covered wooden counter in front of the entrance.

In the distance, from behind the building, came a scratching sound. "What's that?" Dante whispered.

Around the back of the building stood a shadowy figure that appeared to be sweeping or raking the gravel. The group froze, unsure what to do. Dante broke the silence by picking up his walking stick and yelling as he took off toward the figure.

"Wait, Dante!" Damien called.

Used to chasing after Dante, Andy followed them with his camera. Just as Dante was about to beat the figure over the head with his stick, it turned around and blocked his attack with an old handmade broom. Damien ran toward them to see it was a young woman.

"Who the hell are you?" she yelled at them in fluent English with an Australian accent. Her appearance was beautiful but simple, with straight black hair pulled into a low ponytail bound with white paper. Her outfit consisted of a white robe, deep red *hakama*, and pure-white *tabi* covering her feet over black lacquered *geta*. Despite her angry glare, Damien was in awe of her delicate features. Her eyes especially captivated him; they seemed to have a violet hue in the midday sun.

"*Me?*" Dante asked incredulously. "Who are you?" he challenged back.

"Dante, for fuck's sake, drop the stick," Damien said in a hushed voice. "She's a *miko*...a Shinto priestess."

NINE
YOKAI

THE BUILDING along the right side of the main courtyard of the Yamanaka Shinto Shrine served dual roles as the shrine office and a small residential building for Shinto priests and priestesses. Inside this building, Dante, Damien, Mikey, Jen, and Andy sat in a circle on small cushions in a tatami room similar to their room at the inn.

One of the shoji screen doors lining the wall of the room slid open, and Makiko, the Shinto priestess Dante had nearly attacked, entered with a tray. On it was a steaming traditional Japanese teapot and small cups. She knelt on the spare cushion and poured a cup of green tea for each of her guests. "Sorry," she said, handing out each cup. "I thought we had teatime sweets, but I guess not."

"*No, no,*" Damien humbly said in Japanese before switching to English. "This is more than we expected." Judging by her appearance, he guessed Makiko was probably around twenty years old. *She's too young for me*, he thought, but he couldn't help feel smitten by her. He eagerly helped their hostess pass the tea to Jen and Andy on his left. Across from him sat Mikey, then Makiko. Dante sat to his immediate right.

"So," Makiko said, "why are you visiting the shrine?"

"Um...we're in search of a ghost," Dante revealed. "Do you mind if we film an interview with you?"

"Film? Like on camera?" After Dante nodded, she smiled and anxiously combed her fingers through the locks that weren't tied back. "Of course. That's fine."

Both Andy and Jen picked up their cameras and began filming. Again, Dante's persona changed, and he became hellfiredante. "We've made it up the stairs to the Yamanaka Shrine," he explained to their viewers. "This is Makiko, a Shinto priestess here."

"Hi..." She smiled and waved at the cameras.

"So, Makiko, have you ever seen any ghosts in the forest around the shrine?" Dante eagerly asked.

"Of course." She nodded. "The forest surrounding the shine is considered sacred. There's even a sacred stream behind the stalls across the square. They are considered sacred because they are filled with spirits. We ask guests not to wander around the forest because it disturbs the spirits."

Damien and Dante exchanged concerned looks after hearing that last detail.

Noticing their reactions, Makiko grew serious. "Wait. Are you the idiots who have been scaring the spirits in the forest?" Their guilty expressions and silent response told her everything; she sighed in frustration. "You're not supposed to go into the sacred forest. It frightens the spirits."

"B-but we're a ghost-hunting show," Dante countered. "We're on a mission to find a *bakamono*."

"*Baka...?*" Makiko looked at him confused. *Baka* meant *stupid*, but his usage didn't make sense to her. "*Baka **na** mono?*" she asked, questioning if he meant *something stupid*.

Damien put a palm to his face and corrected his friend, "I think you mean *ba**ke**mono*, mate." He turned to Makiko and clarified. "He means we look for *monsters*."

"That's no excuse!" Makiko lectured the group. "If you scare all the ghosts, you will disturb spirits that are much more dangerous. Those are the *real bakemono*. If you value your lives, you need to stay out of the forest, *especially* at night!"

"Wait. That's what Kaz, the innkeeper, also said," Dante remembered. "What happens in the forest at night?"

Makiko stared at him for a moment, seemingly weighing whether to tell him the truth. With a resigned sigh, she continued, "Going into the sacred forest at night will stir up the *yokai*."

"*What?*" Damien's dream about the *kitsune* flashed back in his head. "You mean, like, actual *yokai*? The spirit monsters?" Makiko nodded in response.

This news sent a surge of excitement through Dante. "What kind of *yokai*?"

"Several kinds," Makiko replied. "One you may be familiar with is the *kappa*."

"Wait a minute. Why does that sound familiar?" Mikey asked. He went through the pictures on his phone he'd taken in Nagoya. At one of the rotating sushi restaurants was a cartoon drawing of a turtle with a beak. Showing the picture to Makiko, he continued, "Isn't a *kappa* supposed to be this weird turtle monster? I thought they were just cute mascots."

"Actual *kappa* are much more dangerous," Makiko warned. "They are a child-size, human-like amphibian. They have a dish on their head, a beak for a mouth, and a turtle shell on their back."

"That doesn't sound very dangerous," Dante commented smugly.

"They like to pull their victims into any water source and drown them," Makiko stated. "After they drown their victim, they eat the corpse, starting from the anus."

Again, a surge of excitement went through Dante. Intentional or not, he couldn't pass up this setup. "You mean to tell me there's an actual *yokai* that literally eats ass?"

"Dante!" Damien said.

"But dude! It could literally eat my ass!" Dante said in his boisterous egotistical persona. He smiled. "Think of the content!"

"You'd get banned for that type of content," Mikey warned. Still, he had to admit he found the subject of *yokai* interesting. He turned back to Makiko to his left. "What are some of the other *yokai* here?"

"Hmm..." Makiko thought for a moment. "Oh, the *jubokko*! They're malevolent trees."

"That sounds like some *Evil Dead*–type shit," Damien said under his breath, thinking of the horror movie that was one of the most famous victims of the Video Nasties ban in the United Kingdom in the 1980s. It was before his time but still a popular topic of discussion in his film classes while he was in uni.

Picking up on Damien's comment, Mikey nervously adjusted his glasses and asked Makiko, "Um...do these trees...assault people?"

"Assault?" Makiko looked confused.

"Yeah, like in Tentacle *Hentai*," Dante blurted out, referring to the niche anime porn he'd come across online. If he had any sensible filter, it seemed to have left him when he became hellfiredante.

"Ehhh?" Makiko's eyes opened wide, and her face turned bright red. Scared and embarrassed, she buried her face in her hands.

"Dante!" Jen scolded him from behind the camera.

"What the fuck, mate?" Damien added.

"What? We were all thinking it!" Dante attempted to defend himself. "I didn't make the movie!"

"Still, dude," Andy said with his camera still on him, "have some fucking tact."

"Yada! Sukebei!" Makiko spoke rapidly in Japanese and smacked Dante's right arm.

"Mate, switch places with me." Damien sighed. "She's

calling you a pervert." Dante was going to protest more, but he gave up and just followed Damien's orders.

"Ugh, *kimoi*." Makiko hugged her arms around herself and shuddered.

"That means 'gross,'" Damien whispered to Dante.

"Gee, thanks," Dante whispered back.

Makiko took a deep breath and sighed to calm her nerves. When she was ready, she continued. "No, *jubokko* only trap humans to drain their blood and leave the carcass for animals and insects to consume."

"Still a better way to go than demonic possession," Dante said.

"Dante, shut up!" Jen interrupted him.

"What are some other *yokai*?" Damien asked gently. Remembering his dream, he couldn't resist asking, "Do you see *kitsune*?"

"Oh, yeah. This is an *Inari* shrine, so foxes are supposed to protect the area," Makiko said with a smile. "We also get *jorōgumo*, or I guess it's called, 'The Entangling Bride' in English. *Jorōgumo* are giant spider ladies that like to feed on humans. They especially like to eat young men, so you guys should be careful."

Andy's hands shook. "Fuck, that's terrifying," he muttered. His arachnophobia caused him to freeze at even the tiniest of spiders. The image of a human-size spider was a nightmare worse than any horror movie.

"Are you afraid of spiders?" Jen teased him. "Do you need me to protect you from the spider lady?"

He closed his eyes and shook his head. "I don't know

how much of this shit is real anyway," he replied quietly. "I don't really believe in it."

"The *yokai* you need to be most wary of is the *gashadokuro*, or 'starving skeleton,'" Makiko went on. "*Gashadokuro* is a giant skeleton who likes to bite the heads off humans. It is indestructible and can sneak up on you when it is invisible. The only way you'd know it was around is if you start having a strange ringing in your ears."

"So if you get a ringing in your ears, Dante"—Damien turned back to his friend and smiled—"make sure you run away instead of running toward it."

"Yeah, yeah, yeah," Dante replied with a pout and a dismissive wave of his hand.

Makiko stood in front of the shrine office building and waved goodbye to Dante and his crew. "Bye-bye," she called. "Remember to stay out of the forest!" As the group disappeared down the staircase, she dropped her hand and her smile. "Stupid tourists never listen," she said to herself. Grabbing her broom, she went back to sweeping the autumn leaves in the courtyard.

Heading down the stairs, Dante told Jen and Andy they could stop filming. He knew how difficult it was to film while walking down stairs, and the group didn't need any more injuries. "Did you guys get enough daylight footage?" he asked his cameramen.

Both of them nodded. Then Jen stopped and said,

"What do you mean by 'daylight footage'? Are you still considering going up there at night after all the creepy shit that priestess warned us about?"

"Of course we're going up there at night," Dante argued. "Think about how much of a waste this trip would be if we didn't get nighttime footage." The group was silent in response. Dante tried to rally his troops. "Come on, guys! Japan is one of the safest countries in the world. Do you really think anything will be a big danger to us out here?"

Still no response. The silence forced Dante to question if this really was a good idea. He couldn't run well with his messed-up ankle. Jen and Damien weren't acting like themselves. Everyone was pretty creeped out by the location. And the forest was considered sacred, and it would be incredibly disrespectful to run around it any further.

The content creator in Dante, however, was more concerned about getting nighttime footage to make the episode scary and entertaining. Foolishly he listened to that side of himself instead of any sensible thought. "Get some rest at the inn, guys," he ordered as he continued his climb down the stairs with his walking stick. "Tonight we're going ghost hunting!" For the first time since they'd started filming the show, none of his friends replied with an enthusiastic cheer.

TEN
DANGER

AFTER MIDNIGHT, the group grabbed their equipment for nighttime filming. As they reached the lobby, Dante looked around and found the room empty. Signaling that the coast was clear, he waved for his friends to go out the entrance.

After they left the inn, Kaz opened up one of the shoji screens behind the counter and came in from outside. "*Baka na*," he muttered, and took a drag of his cigarette. They didn't need to sneak out. It wasn't like he was keeping them prisoner. He shook his head. "I was only warning you."

The group found the shrine entrance and climbed the staircase. The stairs up to the shrine were difficult to navigate in the daylight, but in the dark forest at night, it was nearly impossible. Feeling it was unfair for Dante to be the only one with assistance, Andy made him throw away his stick at the entrance. "I saw you run toward that priestess earlier," he said, attempting to justify being rude to his friend.

Once they reached the top, the gravel path that led to the shrine became partially visible as moonlight broke through the heavy clouds. On the less treacherous gravel path, Jen, Andy, and Mikey turned on their cameras and began filming more footage for the show. "All right, guys. Let's get this ghost!" Dante said, pumping his fist in the air. Then his baritone voice took on a suspenseful tone. "Will we find the slit-mouthed woman? Or..." He looked over his shoulder and arched an eyebrow. "...will we find something even more sinister?"

"God, I hope not," Damien commented from beside Dante. Laughing, he tried to hide the uncontrollable shivering in his body. He couldn't tell if the chill in his bones was from the cold or his fear. In an attempt to avoid thinking about it any further, he turned to his friend. "I'm curious to hear if you believe in *yokai*, Dante."

"Hmm..." Dante took a moment to reflect. Jen moved in front of the guys and zoomed in on his face, but his expression was unreadable. The way the beams of moonlight shone down on him, he appeared to have the painted face of a skull. Dante lifted his head to look at the camera, causing the illusion to disappear. "After tonight I think I'll be able to answer that question." He smiled and winked.

"Who knows? Maybe we'll meet the infamous *kappa yokai* that supposedly eats ass!"

"Dante, focus, please," Damien deadpanned. "So where should we go first?" he asked in a hushed tone. He didn't want to risk getting caught by Makiko, especially after she had warned them not to come back to the shrine at night.

"Didn't the priestess say there was a stream?" Mikey asked. "It's supposed to be in the forest behind the festival stalls. Maybe we'll find some spooky footage there?"

The group made their way behind the shrine festival stalls and entered the woods. Andy filmed them from the front as Jen filmed along the right side. Mikey still had his small handheld camera running, this time on night vision so he could see clearer in the forest. Aside from their footsteps on dead leaves and brush, all five members were silent, reflecting the peculiar quiet from the woods surrounding them.

"Isn't a forest supposed to be more active at night?" Damien whispered. He hugged his arms around his body to steady the shaking from his chills. This was a bad idea. *We shouldn't be here*, he thought.

As Mikey watched the woods from the back of the group, through his viewfinder he saw a small figure run from behind a tree. He tried searching the forest with his naked eye, but it was useless; the inky blackness gave nothing away. Taking another step forward, he heard more rustling from the left. "Hey, guys," he called to Dante and the others, who had continued walking. The group turned to look at him. "I heard a noise over there." He pointed toward the forest. "I'm going to go check it out."

"Want us to come with you?" Jen asked, sounding concerned.

"Nah, you guys keep going." Mikey waved them on with a smile. "It'll only take a minute. Besides, we're in Japan. Haunted forest or not, I doubt there's anything really dangerous here."

"Okay, just be careful, bro," Dante said. "Holler if you need us."

It didn't take long for Mikey to lose the lights and sounds of his friends as he made his way deeper into the forest. The night vision on his camera was a godsend. Without it, there was no way he could continue navigating the woods. The video light on the camera was much too dull to use as a flashlight, and the bright light on his mobile phone would probably scare whatever animal he found.

In an attempt to make as little sound as possible, he slowly moved through the moss-covered trees. There was nothing he could do about the crunching of dead leaves under his feet. At least he wasn't charging through the forest and screaming like Dante. He always admired Dante's bravery in the face of fear, but this situation called for stealth, much like one uses when hunting.

Suddenly Mikey heard a rustle, and a child-size figure darted out from a tree a few feet ahead of him. The figure ran ahead at a quick speed. "H-hey, wait!" Mikey yelled, jogging in the direction the figure had gone. "What the hell is a child doing out here in the middle of the night?"

In the viewfinder, Mikey saw a small clearing in the trees and realized he had found the mountain stream. "Whoa," he exclaimed as he tried to stop his momentum. At that moment, he felt something grab his legs, causing him to trip forward. He managed to drop his camera before falling into the stream.

A small but strong figure jumped onto his back and tried to push his face toward the running water. The stream wasn't deep, but Mikey knew it took only an inch of water to drown a human. Whatever had grabbed his legs was now pulling at his jeans, further tangling up his legs. He reached for the figure on his back and managed to grab what felt like a skinny child's wet arm.

"Get the fuck off me!" he yelled and yanked the figure off his back. Fearing for his life, Mikey was able to kick the thing grabbing his legs off him and attempted to stand up to run away. His soaked jeans were now tangled around his knees, causing him to lose his balance. "Damn!" he cursed again as he fell backward into the stream, his glasses disappearing under the muddy water.

That's when he finally heard the grunting of the figure that had been on his back. He looked up to come face-to-face with a four-foot-tall amphibian humanoid. Its green skin looked slimy like a frog's. In place of a mouth was a sharp beak with two nostrils near the top. Dirty, stringy, black hair hung down over its wild eyes. On top of its head was a clear dish that almost looked like a giant bald spot. It was an actual *kappa*!

"Oh, come on! Dante's the one who wanted his ass eaten," Mikey whined.

The *kappa* in front of him reached out and grabbed his shoulders. No longer able to suppress his fear, he let out a deep guttural scream just as the *kappa* shoved him face-first into the stream water. He struggled against the creature's inhuman strength. The second *kappa* took the advantage, grabbing hold of his wrists and pulling them back so he was unable to use him arms to push himself up.

Within seconds, Mikey became overwhelmed by the cold water and the mud of the stream. Unable to hold his breath, he felt the water and mud slide into his nose and mouth. Terror and panic turned to resignation. In his last moments, he thought of his wife and infant son. *I'm sorry, Kate.* Hot tears stung his closed eyes in contrast to the chilly stream water. *I'm so sorry I won't be there to help you raise Charlie.* Finally, his body became still then went limp. The two *kappa* celebrated capturing their dinner by letting out victory grunts into the cold night air.

ELEVEN
NO SIGNAL

MIKEY'S guttural scream echoed throughout the forest before becoming garbled by water. The pained sound startled Dante and the others. They stared at one another, taking a moment to register that their friend was in trouble.

"Mikey!" Jen shouted in a panic.

The four of them made their way through the forest as quickly as they could, dodging trees, dead brush, slippery moss, and exposed roots. Navigating through the thick woods, Jen and Andy used the mounted video lights on their cameras as flashlights.

"Where did the sound coming from?" Dante huffed. A swollen lump of fear for his friend was growing in his throat.

"Down this way," Jen replied, out of breath. She pointed diagonally toward where Mikey had entered the woods. The group followed her directions, eventually reaching a stream.

"Isn't this the mountain stream?" Damien asked, trying to hide the shivering in his voice.

"It sounded like the scream became garbled," Andy reminded everyone. They looked at one another and ran down the bank of the stream.

Soon they came across an object obstructing the stream. Two animals on the object noticed the crew and scurried away. As the group approached, they saw it was a man on his knees, face down in the river. The body had its jeans around the knees and its underwear partially pulled down, exposing its rear.

"Jesus Christ!" exclaimed Dante as he ran toward the body.

Jen, Andy, and Damien followed. As they closed in on body, the four friends noticed the animals that were on the corpse had appeared to be eating it from the anus. Jen gasped and looked away. Andy vomited on the forest floor.

A terrifying chill ran down Damien's spine as he recognized the dark-green *Ghost Theories* merch jacket on the body. "M-mikey?" he asked in disbelief.

"*What?*" Dante turned to him in disbelief. "No way! This has to be a prank!"

"Dante, it's Mikey's jacket," Damien pointed out.

Dante shook his head. "No." He couldn't believe his eyes. "Which one of you is pranking us? Where's Mikey?" he shouted at the others.

"He's right there, Dante," Jen cried. She took a breath. "We need to move him."

"*What?*" Andy grabbed her by the right shoulder and

shook her. "No fucking way, Jen! What the fuck are we going to do when the police get here? You can't move a dead body!"

"So what should we do then?" she shouted back at Andy. "Should we just leave him in this embarrassing pose to be eaten by whatever those animals were?" She wiped her tears away with the sleeve of her red flannel coat. "We can't leave Mikey like this!"

Dante took a breath. "Guys, we're not doing any good by yelling at each other," he said calmly. "Jen, head back to the gravel path to see if you can call 911."

"It's 119 in Japan," Damien quietly corrected him.

"119," Dante confirmed with a nod and turned back to Jen. "If you can't get a signal, go to the *ryokan* and see if they can phone an ambulance," he ordered. "And be careful, please." Jen nodded and turned to make her way back out of the forest.

The three remaining friends fell into an uncomfortable silence. None of them could bring themselves to look at Mikey's body. Damien suddenly thought about Makiko staying on her own at the shrine office. What if whatever attacked Mikey decided to go after her? "I should go warn Makiko," he decided.

"Jesus fucking Christ, would you stop thinking with your dick for one second?" Andy snapped at him. "Quit being a fucking simp for that girl just because she's Japanese!"

"What the fuck? You're one to talk, you fucking wanker!" Damien yelled at him. "At least I'm not screwing around with my best friend's ex-girlfriend behind his back!"

Pissed off, Andy got in Damien's face. "What the fuck did you just say?"

"You heard me," Damien spat. "Mikey knew too. Maybe you're the one who set this up to get rid of him!"

Both men started to scuffle. Before it could get worse, Dante got between his two friends and pushed them apart. "Hey! Stop it!" he yelled. He looked to Damien. "Go tell Makiko something happened to Mikey and see if she has a phone," he instructed him. Damien fixed his disheveled clothes and ran off toward the shrine.

After Damien was out of sight, Dante looked to Andy. "Is it true?" he asked quietly.

Andy shook his head and sighed. "Look, Dante..." he replied. "Jen was going to tell you after we got ba—" He was cut off by a mean left hook to the nose. He doubled over and placed a hand on a nearby tree to steady himself.

Dante shook out his left hand. He wasn't used to bare-knuckle boxing, but fuck did that feel good. "If Jen wants to date you, fine. She's an adult—she can make her own decisions," he said, and pointed to Andy. "But wait until she's moved out of my place! Understood?"

"Yeah," Andy said, still dazed. *Don't fuck with a guy who's been training for a charity boxing event*, he thought. He put a finger underneath his nose to check if it was bleeding. Sure enough, he saw thick dark liquid on his fingers when he pulled them away. "Fuck," he muttered, and pulled a tissue out of his pocket to stop the bleeding. Next to the tree he was leaning on, he noticed a small red light glowing. "Hey, wait a minute!" He crouched then stood up holding something black in his hand. "I think this is Mikey's handheld camera."

"*What?*" Dante replied and took the camera from Andy. He looked it over. On the bottom of the camcorder was a label stating, "Property of M. I. Witt." He took a nervous breath, "Do you think this recorded what happened to him?"

Andy shrugged. It was a possibility, but neither friend could bring himself to rewind the footage to find out. "I'll hang on to it for now," Dante decided.

Southeast of Dante and Andy, Jen finally emerged from the dark forest to find the gravel path. The woods were a formidable foe; the sparse moonlight offered no sense of direction either. Thankfully that didn't stop her from finding an escape. As soon as she was out, she checked her phone but saw she had no signal.

"Jesus Christ, Dante," Jen breathed. "Why did you have to choose this place?" Of course the location was so remote that her mobile phone wouldn't get a signal. *I thought Japan was supposed to be technologically advanced.* Who would believe there were places where you still couldn't get a signal?

Minutes later, Jen recognized the two lion dog statues, indicating she was almost to the stairs. At that moment, she heard a sudden high-pitched ringing in her right ear. "Ow," she whined, and was about to look over her right shoulder to see if something was following her. Just as suddenly as the sound came, it subsided as she passed the lion dog statues. *That's funny*, she thought, rubbing her ear. She glanced back but found nothing in the moonlight.

Another few steps forward, and she reached the staircase that led down to the road. "Thank God," she said, and gingerly took a step down. The stairs felt even more treacherous going down, especially at night. A beep sounded, causing her to jump. Looking down, she saw her camera was still on and beeping at her with a low-battery warning. "The heck," Jen muttered. She was trying to find the power button as she continued to descend the stairs.

When she nearly reached the platform, she heard creaking in the forest surrounding her. It sounded as if the branches were being blown by a strong wind, except there was no wind. She held her breath and scanned the forest for movement. Maybe whatever had gotten Mikey was now after her. Suddenly a tree branch whipped against her back, slicing the back of her flannel jacket open like a bullwhip. The impact forced her to stumble toward the limbs of the tree that had entangled her earlier in the afternoon. Terrified, she screamed and dropped her camera, which rolled off the stairs and into the brush.

Jen struggled against the branches, which felt like claws intentionally pulling her by her hair. "Come on," she pleaded with tears in her eyes. "Please let me go!" Instead of cooperating, the long, sharp branches tightened their grip around her head. In the gaps between the dark twigs, she saw the trunk of the large tree crack and open. Inside was a hollow tomb with several wooden spikes, resembling an iron maiden.

"No!" she screamed in protest. Without hesitation, the tree unceremoniously threw her into the spiky cavity. "Help me!" Jen desperately screamed for the last time before the trunk closed around her, entombing her inside. Dark streams of blood poured like sap down the trunk before becoming absorbed into the bark.

Dante and Andy froze at the sound of Jen's screams. They looked at each other, unsure what to do. "Go help her!" Dante ordered Andy. "I'll go get Damien," he decided. "We need to get the hell out of here!

"All right." Andy nodded in agreement.

"Don't wait for us." Dante glared at his friend. "Once you find Jen, get the fuck out of here. Understood?"

"Yes," Andy said. "Be careful, Dante," he added quietly before he turned and ran in the direction Jen had gone.

"You too," Dante replied, fully aware his friend could no longer hear him. He sighed and set off in the direction Damien had gone. Looking at Mike's camcorder in his hands, he checked to make sure it was recording and used the night vision to navigate his way through the forest.

"This is Dante Anderson," he started narrating, "and I'm at the sacred forest of the Yamanaka Shinto Shrine."

Talking to himself was a coping skill he'd learned while playing horror games. Now it was acting as a coping mechanism for the horrific situation he was currently in. "I don't know what the fuck is going on," he said, "but my friends and I are in grave danger."

TWELVE
NIGHTMARE

HAVING experience as a cross country runner in high school, Andy easily jogged through the forest, jumping over roots and branches that could potentially trip him. "Jen! Where are you?" he called into the dark woods. There was no response. "Fuck," he muttered, but he refused to give up. Not much time had passed since he and Dante had heard her screaming; she should still be in the area.

Using his camcorder as his flashlight, he continued to search through the forest. It was a good thing Dante had reminded him to charge his battery earlier. "Dante," he said, sighing. *I royally fucked over one of my oldest friendships for a girl, didn't I?* It would be all for naught if he couldn't find her.

"Jen?" he called out. "Jennifer White, are you there?" Just as the trees and shrubs were about to clear, indicating he was near the gravel path, Andy heard a rustling sound in the bushes behind him. Flashing his light over, he tried calling out again: "Jennifer, can you hear me?" *Did she not make it to the path?*

Then he heard it faintly echoing in the distance, deep within the woods. It was Jen's voice screaming, "Help me!" Andy's heart pounded with hope, and he took off like a lightning bolt.

Soon he returned to the mountain stream. It must've been downstream from where Mikey had died. Traces of blood were running in the water. *Did she come back this way?* he asked himself. Jen didn't seem to be *that* directionally challenged. Wouldn't she realize the staircase was in the opposite direction?

"Help me!" he heard her screaming again. It was across the stream, farther into the woods. At least it sounded closer.

Andy jumped across the stream and jogged in the direction of the voice. Maybe something had dragged her in this direction? It would explain why she was still screaming, right? He continued running until he reached the mouth of a cave. Next to the cave was a tall dead tree with outstretched limbs that created a canopy over the entrance. High up in the branches, he finally found Jen. "Help me!" she screamed again.

"Jen!" Andy shouted, and ran to the tree. "Hold on! I'll get you down!" he yelled up to her. After placing his camcorder on the ground near the tree, he took a running start and jumped up to grab a low-hanging branch. There was a creak in the old dead wood as it took on all 190 pounds of his weight. Unable to withstand the strain, the branch snapped off and he fell to the ground, landing flat on his back. The impact knocked the wind out of his lungs, causing him to gasp for breath.

"Help me!" Jen screamed again, frantically.

"Jesus, I fucking heard you," he muttered as he sat up and rubbed the back of his head. Blades of grass and a few small twigs shook loose from his curly hair. Hopefully he didn't have a concussion; that type of injury could kill a person. Slowly he got up from the ground and picked a different branch to start with. Not using a running start this time, he reached up to a large, thick branch and climbed, staying close to the trunk.

As he got closer, Jen desperately reached out to him. It looked like her legs were stuck in something, but he couldn't make out what it was in the dark. "Hold on," he said as he continued to climb. "I'm almost there."

Finally he grabbed the large branch she was on and pulled himself up. Immediately she wrapped her arms around him in a tight hug and buried her face against his neck. "Shh, it's okay, babe," Andy tried to comfort her. He rubbed her back with his right hand and noticed a large, bulbous shape starting from her waist.

Curious, he looked over her shoulder to see the lower half of a human-size spider. Yellow and blue stripes marked the back of the gigantic insect body. A hint of red appeared to line the abdomen. Eight impossibly long black spider legs marked with matching yellow stripes stretched out from the creature's sides. Upon closer inspection, he noticed a massive web of golden threads stretched between the dead branches.

"F-fuck!" he breathed. A lifetime's worth of arachnophobia culminated to this point where he was face-to-face with an enormous spider lady. His palms became sweaty, and he tried to let go, preferring to fall to the ground instead of further embracing this creature. It was too late, though. In addition to her human arms, the Jen copy had her eight spider legs wrapped around Andy's body and was making quick work to wrap him in a cocoon of golden webs. Fear stole his voice, and he couldn't even let out a scream to wake him up from this nightmare.

The spider lady giggled as she held him tightly against her. The sound was completely different from the flirtatious giggling Jen always gave him. This was a hollow, unnatural sound that left him feeling cold and terrified.

Suddenly he felt a sharp prick in his neck, and the cold, cruel reality of his situation hit him. He was going to die here, at the disgusting hands and legs of this freak monster. A wave of paralysis radiated from the bite mark throughout the rest of his body.

Although Andy was no longer able to move, he still felt a strange tugging sensation on his body. He closed his eyes, wishing his death would be quick. Unfortunately, just before his mind surrendered to paralysis, he remembered Makiko's words that the *jorōgumo* liked to feed on young men. If this thing behaved like a true spider, Andy was most likely being wrapped up to be savored as a living food source for several days. With a helpless dread, he knew this would be a slow, agonizing death.

On the ground beneath Andy's wrapped, hanging corpse, a black-winged creature landed with a soft thud. The being stood up, revealing a manlike creature dressed in a Buddhist priest's garb, complete with a pom-pom sash over his white robe, red *hakama*, and one-toothed *geta* sandals. A small black cap sat on top of his head. Underneath the cap, his long brown hair was tied back in a low ponytail.

The creature looked up to reveal a red monster mask with long nose in the moonlight. Seeing the corpse in the tree, he shook his head and pulled out a cast iron *kiseru*, a long traditional Japanese pipe. He filled it with finely shredded tobacco and lit it, taking a deep inhalation from the mouthpiece. As he exhaled, he looked back up at the corpse in the tree again. "Damn it," he said in a deep, raspy voice.

"*Ya, ya, tengu-kun,*" a haggard old lady croaked as she appeared beside him. She was the local *yamauba*, or mountain witch, who was known to wander around the area. Silvery hair was piled on her head, resembling a bird's nest. Her worn yellow kimono was faded and frayed at the hem. On her feet were dirty white *tabi* socks and straw sandals. Years of wear and tear on her ancient body had caused her to be permanently hunched over. Her wrinkly face turned to the side and upward to see the hanging corpse wrapped in spiderwebs. "Ah, it looks like the *jorōgumo* is going to eat well for a while," she said in Japanese.

"Yeah, unfortunately," the *tengu* replied. He blew out another puff of smoke. "Foolish humans. I tried to warn them."

"It's not your fault, Kazuya-kun." The *yamauba* cackled. "At least you tried." Looking back down at the ground, she noticed a device next to the base of the tree. "Eh? What's that?" she asked, pointing to the unfamiliar technology.

Recognizing the camcorder, Kaz leaned down and picked it up. "It's one of their cameras," he replied. Although he recognized who it belonged to, he wasn't familiar with how it worked. "Yuki-san," he said, addressing the *yamauba*. "Would you mind placing this near the road? And if you come across any other cameras, keep them together."

The old lady gave him a suspicious look and took the camera. "Are you sure?" she asked in a low voice. Her lips pursed, revealing wrinkles around her mouth that resembled skeleton teeth.

Kaz nodded with certainty. "You know we won't show up on the footage," he commented. Over the years, he had learned that *yokai* would resemble shadows in videos but weren't actually visible unless they wanted to be. "Besides, it doesn't belong to us."

Yuki nodded in agreement and disappeared in a puff of purple smoke. Kazuya lifted his left foot and banged his pipe on the bottom sole of his sandal. Gray ashes fell out only to be carried away on a strong breeze. "Time to get back," he said to himself, as his large black wings carried him into the dark night sky.

Several Minutes Earlier

Damien burst out of the forest and ran around the festival stalls into the large square of the shrine. His black Chuck Taylors skidded across the gravel. His gaze darted ahead as he checked to see if there were any lights on in the shrine office building. The building, however, was completely dark. Regardless, he jumped over the information counter, ran to the sliding entrance door, and pounded on it. "Makiko! Makiko can you hear me? It's Damien!"

"Yeah, you're loud enough to wake the dead," Makiko complained as she came around the corner of the building and walked back behind the counter. "And stop pounding on the door! You're going to break it!"

"Oh, thank God!" Damien exclaimed, and hugged her. She froze and quickly pushed him away. "Sorry. I'm just so relieved you're okay."

"Why wouldn't I be?" she asked, her eyebrows scrunching together.

Damien was still out of breath. "My...my friend Mikey is dead. We found his body in the stream. Some animals were eating his corpse from the anus."

"The *kappa*," Makiko said with a whisper of disbelief.

She closed her eyes and rubbed her temples. "I told you idiots not to come back up here after dark."

"I..." At a loss for words, Damien paused. "I know, but..." At that moment, a woman's scream from the path south of the shrine interrupted him. He recognized it immediately. "Oh, no! Jen!" Just as he was about to run in the direction of the scream, he nearly tripped backward. Makiko was hanging on to his left wrist with a terrified look in her eyes; her grip felt unnaturally strong.

"Please," she pleaded. "Please don't leave me! I'm afraid to be alone!"

Conflicted, Damien looked toward the gate then back toward Makiko. *If I heard Jen screaming, Dante and Andy probably heard her too, right?* He bit his bottom lip, took a deep breath, and exhaled. "Okay." He nodded. "I'll stay here with you."

Makiko sighed with relief. "Thank you," she said, still hanging on to his wrist. "Now let's get inside before we get any unwanted visitors!" She pulled him to the door of the shrine office and slid it open.

Damien looked at her in disbelief. "You don't keep it locked?"

"Normally there wouldn't be anyone at the shrine at this hour," Makiko explained as she pulled him inside the building.

Dante slowly made his way through the forest toward the gravel path. Periodically he checked the viewfinder of Mikey's camcorder to see if the night-vision function would reveal any predators or obstacles. "I didn't plan for this to happen," he said, communicating his thoughts to his future viewers as he navigated around moss-covered trees. "I mean...who'd believe *yokai* actually exist? Am I right?" His sardonic laughter reverberated throughout the woods, surprising even himself. He froze, afraid he was making too much noise.

The moment of silence struck a somber note. After a minute, he took a deep breath and slowly continued forward. "Man, why did it have to be Mikey?" he said quietly. He shook his head, "I mean, I wouldn't want any of my friends to get hurt, but...Mikey was such a nice guy and he had a family." His eyes felt misty, and he quickly wiped away a tear before it could fully form. "He was a good friend. He definitely didn't deserve to go out in such a horrific way."

Dante stopped in his tracks as his monologue was interrupted by a strange chirping sound. "What's that?" he whispered into the camera's microphone. He scanned the area with his eyes and the camcorder. The sound wasn't something a bird would make...unless there were bird *yokai*. The thought made his whole body shiver with fear.

Another chirping sound came from high up in the trees. "Shit," Dante cursed under his breath. He swung the camera upward and looked around. A pair of eyes glowed in the viewfinder. Soon more eyes appeared, accompanied by several chirps. The dull flashlight on the camera illuminated several red faces. Dante let out a horrified scream and ran off, continuing toward the shrine. Up in the trees, a troop of Japanese snow monkeys watched the strange human run away. With the threat of danger no longer present, the monkeys stopped chirping and went back to sleep.

THIRTEEN
SWEETHEART

BACK IN THE shrine administrative building, Damien and Makiko sat next to each other in the dark tatami room. It didn't feel as peaceful at night as it had been during the day, when he and his friends were casually drinking green tea and listening to Makiko talk about *yokai*. That moment felt like ages ago.

"Are you sure we can't turn on the lights...or a portable heater?" Damien asked. He crossed his arms in front of his chest, unconsciously expressing his discomfort. The shadows in the corners of the room seemed to be concealing angry spirits. He laughed to himself. *Who knew a guy who plays horror games for a living would be afraid of the dark?*

"Do you want to risk letting the other *yokai* know we're in here?" Makiko replied tensely. Damien flinched in response. Looking remorseful, Makiko sighed and her expression softened. "Do you want me to tell you a story to distract you?"

"Yes, please." Damien nodded. "I'd like that."

"Okay, so I know you and your friends came here looking for the *kuchisake onna*, but the ghost story people are familiar with ends too quickly," Makiko said in a hushed, animated voice. "The story doesn't tell the tale of what happened to the innkeeper's daughter after her father dedicated his life to caring for this shrine."

Damien tilted his head in confusion like a puppy. His blue eyes shone brightly even in the dark room. "Didn't she die?"

"Yes, but do you believe her spirit could rest peacefully in that well?" Makiko argued.

Damien frowned. "I suppose not."

Makiko looked wistfully around the dark room. "That innkeeper spent the rest of his eighty-year life caring for this shrine to repent for what he did to his daughter," she continued. "The Shinto *kami*—"

"Gods?" Damien interrupted her.

"Yes. The Shinto *kami* were so impressed with the man's dedication that when he died, they offered to turn his daughter's restless spirit into a *kitsune* to guard the shrine."

"The nine-tailed fox *yokai*?" Damien asked in disbelief. Makiko nodded. "I can't believe it," he said quietly. "During the drive here, I had a weird dream that a *kitsune* was waiting for me."

Makiko gave him a gentle smile and leaned over to whisper in his ear, "*Zutto matteita ne.*"

I've been waiting. Damien immediately understood what she'd said in Japanese. Fear gripped his heart as he realized he recognized the voice from his dream. He turned his head to look at her and scrambled backward. "Bloody hell!" he screamed.

Makiko covered her mouth and giggled. Despite the darkness, her white fox ears and nine tails were now clearly visible. Two long silver scars appeared on the sides of her mouth where she had been cut as a young woman. Her eyes emanated an unnatural magenta glow. There was no denying it: she was the *kuchisake onna and* a *kitsune yokai*.

"Fuck," Damien muttered, his heart beating with a sickening thud. "Wh—" He took a panicky breath. "What are you going to do? Are you going to kill me?"

"Hmm..." Makiko put a finger to her chin as she pondered his questions. Her once neatly manicured nails had grown into long black claws. "Normally I would say no. I mean, *kitsune* are not known to be as violent as the Korean *kumiho* nine-tailed fox spirit."

"But..." Damien urged her to continue.

"But..." Makiko grinned at him. "I haven't eaten in over a month. I'm pretty hungry."

"What did you eat last?" Damien asked. He was trying to keep her talking as he gradually backed away. The more he stalled, the more time he had to either be found by his friends or somehow escape. His eyes darted around the room, trying to find a way out.

"An Australian photographer came through a couple months ago." Makiko laughed. The eerie sound immobilized Damien. "The *tengu* was pretty angry with him for wandering around in the forest at night after he had explicitly warned him not to."

"Wait," Damien rasped breathlessly. It was like the nightmares where he wanted to scream but no sound would come out of his throat. "Your accent..."

"Yeah, it was his." She grinned again. "Do you like it?" She started crawling toward him on her hands and knees. Slowly Damien backed up until he bumped into the shoji screen wall. "I must say I'd be happy to switch it up, though." She closed in on him. "I've always wanted an English accent," she added, then dived toward him.

In the polished hallway outside the room, long black claws penetrated the shoji screen. The old paper appeared to blush deep crimson as Damien's blood soaked into the screen. As Makiko forcibly pulled her hand back, she grabbed his heart, ripping it out of his chest. Dark red fluid splattered across the walls and the tatami floor. Damien's lifeless body collapsed sideways to the floor with a dull thud.

After taking a large bite out of the still-warm human heart in her hands, Makiko let out a satisfied hum from her throat. "As expected." She smiled, revealing bright-white fangs through her blood-covered mouth. "Sweet hearts really do taste the best."

Still terrified of his encounter with the red-faced monsters in the trees, and unaware these monsters were actually snow monkeys, Dante continued to run until he was out of the forest. When he emerged from the woods, he paused for a moment to get his bearings. His ankle was killing him from the unexpected strain. Ahead of him, he saw the large gravel square of the shrine and the administrative building across the way.

Without a second thought, he quickly hobbled toward the building and climbed across the wooden counter where the shrine attendants sold talismans to visitors. He stumbled and rolled across the floor inside the stall, landing in front of the door to the building. He picked up his camera and was about to knock on the door when he heard a rustling noise from the woods.

"Fuck," he uttered, and immediately attempted to open the door. The door easily slid open, nearly knocking him off balance. Not wanting to tempt fate into having him meet whatever was making noise in the forest, Dante scrambled inside the building and closed the door.

As soon as he crawled inside the tatami room, he closed his eyes and leaned his forehead against the doorframe. "Jesus," he muttered, out of breath. His black eyes slowly opened and searched the room behind him, but it was too dark to see. The corners were completely covered in shadow. If anyone was in the room with him, Dante wouldn't have had a clue.

Remembering Mikey's camera, he looked around the room through the viewfinder. In the back corner, he spotted a large motionless object on the floor. *Shit.* He let out a frustrated sigh and stood up. Walking to the center of the room, he felt around for the overhead light he had noticed during the day. The switch cord swung around as it hit the back of his hand. Finally he managed to grasp the string and pulled.

The single florescent ring light illuminated with a buzz underneath a square paper lampshade. Exhausted, Dante squinted until his eyes could adjust to the harsh light. He blinked then frowned at what he saw. The motionless object was a body. Blood covered the corpse and was seeping into the tatami mat flooring. "Oh, no, no," he said, recognizing the dark-blue hoodie and black Chuck Taylors. "Not you too, Damien." Slowly he approached his best friend's body. In Damien's chest was a bloody hole the size of a large fist. Whatever had attacked him appeared to have ripped out his heart.

"Fuck," Dante cursed again, then sat down next to his friend. Damien's once-bright-blue eyes were now faded and lifeless. Blood matted his sandy-blond hair, and his pale skin had turned ashen with death. Weary, Dante placed the handheld camera next to him, pulled his knees up to his chest, rested his elbows on his knees, and put his head in his hands. The exhaustion, pain, and loneliness overwhelmed him. "I'm so sorry we came here," he sobbed quietly. "Please...please forgive me."

Suddenly there was a large rumble and the building shook. Dante picked his head up and looked around wildly. *An earthquake?* After scrambling to his feet, he grabbed the camcorder and raced out of the room. Once outside, he climbed over the wooden counter of the administrative building and ran into the square. Dante scanned the area, but nothing appeared to have been damaged or shaken out of place. So what had caused the tremor? And why was his tinnitus getting unbearably louder? "Dante," he heard Damien's voice whisper in his right ear over the loud ringing.

At that moment, the clouds cleared, and the bright full moon shone with all its might. The white moonlight illuminated the square, and that's when Dante finally saw it. A massive demonic skeleton was leaning over him. It was the *gashadokuro*, the starving skeleton. Deep in its black eye sockets was a faint red glow that was growing stronger. The creature let out a low moan, sending an icy wave across the square. In his ear, Dante heard his friend whisper to him again, this time with urgency: "Run!"

FOURTEEN
RUN

FUELED by a surge of fear-driven adrenaline, Dante turned and sprinted toward the gates of the shrine. For the first time in his adult life, he was running away, but with good reason. As crazy and unimaginable as the monsters were that *possibly* had murdered his friends, he reminded himself this wasn't a video game. There were no second chances if he failed to get away from the giant skeleton behind him.

The first stone torii gate grew larger as Dante ran toward it. Maybe he'd gone far enough? Maybe he could risk taking a look back at the insane monster he'd probably never see again in his lifetime? His pace slowed only a fraction of a second, just in time for a large skeletal hand to slam down around him. Dante opened his eyes and found he was right between the splayed index and middle fingers of the *gashadokuro*'s left hand.

Nope. There was no use looking back at a once-in-a-lifetime monster if it meant cutting his life short. If Dante weren't out of breath, he would have screamed. Instead he let out a whine and cried out, "What the fuck?" The huge skeleton didn't seem to appreciate his elusiveness. A large growl rattled through the bones of its rib cage and vibrated into the ground. The huge bony fingers tried to close around the body of its prey. "Shit!" Dante exclaimed, then ran at full speed out of the creature's grasp and through the stone gate. The *gashadokuro* responded by letting out a frustrated grunt and slowly started to get to its feet.

Dante dashed down the gravel path toward the staircase that led to the road. His lungs burned and his ankle ached, but he had to get out of there. Suddenly a colossal skeleton foot came down, crushing the guardian lion dog statue right next to him. "Fuck!" Damien screamed, and immediately coughed. He stumbled toward the staircase.

As Dante passed through the torii gate, the monster's left foot came down at the edge of the shrine's path. The ground rumbled, knocking him off balance. He fell down the first set of stairs and hit another gate at the landing, where the stairs changed direction. The impact caused him to drop Mikey's handheld camera. The camcorder fell into the steep wooded area and rolled out of view.

Perhaps it was a strong instinct toward self-preservation, but Dante managed to remain conscious after his fall. Although he was battered and out of breath, he was awake. "Get up," he muttered, willing his body to move when it no longer wanted to. As he got to his feet, a sharp pain shot through his left foot and radiated up his leg. "Gah!" he cried out, and picked his foot back up.

From behind him came a deep, low grumbling. Was that thing actually following him outside of the shrine grounds? Preferring survival over getting killed by curiosity, Dante hobbled down the staircase as quickly as he could, grabbing on to every torii gate that arched over the path. A string of painful curses accompanied every step.

Finally he made it to the second landing, where the stairs changed direction a final time. It indicated he was nearly at the road. He heard a female voice yell at him in his head: *Leave!* As he stepped off the landing, two icy cold hands forcefully pushed his back, causing him to tumble down the remaining stairs.

Dante opened his eyes to find he was now lying face down in the gravel beside the road at the base of the Yamanaka shrine staircase. He didn't know how long he had been unconscious. It could have been a few seconds or several minutes. A long wooden object next to him caught his attention. It was the stick Andy had made him discard earlier. Using it to pull himself to standing, Dante took a deep breath and hobbled back toward the *ryokan*.

Headlights suddenly illuminated the area as a van came up the mountain road. Dante squinted as the right driver's-side window rolled down just a crack. "What the hell?" A familiar voice came from the window. "Hey, Eric! Look, it's Dante!"

"No way," Dante mumbled.

"Dante? What the hell are you doing here, man?" The van door opened, and he recognized the round face with a scruffy mustache that covered the top lip and the chin-length, bleached blond hair. It was his friend and fellow content creator, Eric Ross, one half of the comedy duo the Two Dingle Buds.

The other half of the duo was Joshua Davis, whom Dante now recognized as the owner of the first voice he'd heard. Josh was driving the vehicle. His dark-brown skin and friendly smile came into view as he fully rolled down the tinted window. "Hey, man, are you okay? You look pretty beaten up."

"You have no idea," Dante said quietly. If he didn't have his stick to lean on, he would've collapsed from the exhaustion. "What are you guys doing here?"

"We're on tour in Japan," Eric said with a boastful smile. "We had a day between our shows in Nagoya and Osaka, so we were going to stop at the *ryokan* up ahead to rest for the night."

"No shit." Dante chuckled. He couldn't believe his luck. "Can you give me a ride? That's where we're staying."

"You and who?" Josh asked.

Dante frowned, realizing he was alone. There was no telling if Andy or Jen had made it out of the forest, but considering what had happened to Mikey and Damien, Dante wasn't feeling optimistic. With a shiver, he looked back at the woods that had claimed the lives of at least two of his friends. Almost as if in reply, the woods rustled back at him and a loud piercing tone rang in his ears.

Quickly turning back to the van, Dante urgently hopped in. "I'll explain when we reach the inn," he said, slamming the sliding door shut. "But right now we need to get out of here."

At the *ryokan*, Dante sat in one of the comfy armchairs in the lobby. Kneeling in front of him was Kaz, who examined Dante's foot and gave his guest a disappointed look. "I think it's broken," he said as he got to his feet. He pulled out a cigarette from the pack in his track suit pants pocket and placed it between his lips. "I told you not to go into the forest after dark," he mumbled as he lit his cigarette.

"Wow! An innkeeper *and* a doctor! You're a man of many talents," Dante replied sarcastically. He knew he should be grateful, but he couldn't shake the gnawing feeling that Kaz knew exactly what monsters lurked around the Yamanaka shrine. What if he was assigned with the task of feeding tourists to the *yokai*? What if he actually *was* a *yokai*?

Almost as if reading his mind, Kaz rolled his eyes. "Any damn fool can see it's broken," he said, pointing to Dante's foot. He exhaled, blowing out a thick hazy cloud of smoke, and picked up the receiver of the green phone at the front desk. "I'm going to call an ambulance," he explained before dialing 119.

"You should probably call the police," Dante retorted.

Kaz gave him a dead-eyed stare, then turned his attention back to the phone. "Ah, *moshi moshi*," he said to the emergency operator before relaying the situation in Japanese much too fast for Dante to follow.

While Kaz was on the phone, Eric and Josh approached Dante. They had just finished getting settled into their rooms with their crew. Eric, the younger and more immature one of the duo, glanced at the innkeeper on the phone and turned back to Dante. "What's going on?" he whispered.

Still feeling suspicious, Dante gestured for both Josh and Eric to come in closer. "He's calling an ambulance," he said in a hushed voice. He sighed and closed his eyes. "Look, I don't think anyone is going to believe me, but there are monsters up at that shrine," he stated. "Monsters that attacked me and murdered my friends Mikey and Damien. I'm suspecting they got Jen and Andy too, but I'm not sure."

"So what do you want us to do?" Josh asked with a concerned look. Dante wasn't as close to him as he was to Eric, but in the various times he'd met him, it never seemed like he was crazy.

"We had three camcorders," Dante replied. "Two professional ones and a handheld one Mikey had." He took a breath, aware that what he was going to ask could endanger both of them. "Please..." He looked to them. "Please at least find the small camera and promise me you'll send the footage to my editor, Allie. Here's her card with her info." He fished a card out of his wallet and handed it to Josh.

Josh and Eric looked at each other. Josh was the older and more cautious one of the two. He sighed and asked his partner, "What do you think, man?"

Eric frowned. He didn't fully believe Dante's story, but something must have happened at the shrine to leave him in this mental state and with a broken foot. The curiosity was eating away at him. "Okay, fine," he finally replied. "We'll go look for Jen and Andy, at least. If we find the camera, you can rely on us to send the footage."

For the first time since they'd picked him up alongside the mountain road, they saw a wave of relief come across Dante's face. "Thank you," he said. The sincerity in his voice was off-putting for Eric and Josh. This wasn't the confident, boisterous Dante Anderson they'd come to know over the years. This Dante had *definitely* seen some shit tonight.

While Kaz was on the phone with the operator, Josh and Eric slipped out of the lobby to make their way toward the shrine. Dante closed his eyes and rested his head on the back of the soft, oversize chair. There was nothing more he could do; it was all up to the Two Dingle Buds to get the truth out now. He chuckled. "I'm fucked," he mumbled before dozing off to sleep.

FIFTEEN
FOUND FOOTAGE

THE TWO DINGLE Buds had been together on VidTV for eight years and friends for nearly twenty. Eric and Josh originally had met in high school and bonded over shows like *Mystery Science Theater 3000* and *Space Ghost Coast to Coast*. Recognizing they had the same comedy style, the two friends had come up with the idea for their show while attending college. When VidTV became popular, they created their weekly parody show where they reviewed various products, reacted to viral videos, and invited guest content creators to join in. Although they got their start on VidTV, they were now more known for their comedy tours and live shows.

Eric and Josh silently walked down the mountain road. Only the sounds of their footsteps accompanied them in the cold night air. They still couldn't believe what Dante had told them. Damien Knight and Mikey Witt had been murdered at the shrine they were currently walking toward. Were they risking their lives just to look for a camera?

Josh shivered at the realization. "What the fuck are we doing?"

"We're walking down a quiet mountain road in Japan at three in the morning," Eric replied matter-of-factly.

"I know that!" Josh snapped, then took a moment to calm down. The silence of the creepy forest around them was putting him on edge. He let out a deep breath. "I mean, what are we doing this for? What if we get killed too?"

Eric took a moment to piece his thoughts together. "I... don't know if I fully believe Dante's story, but I still wanted to help the guy. You saw how messed up he was. Plus, in the van earlier, he mentioned how *kappa* supposedly eat ass... like literally!"

"Eric, I need you to focus, please," Josh replied with a small laugh. Although he never expressed it verbally, he was always thankful for Eric's small comedic interruptions. As he looked up ahead, a shadowy figure formed in the dense fog. He nudged his best friend with his elbow. "Hey, what's that?"

"What?" Eric responded, squinting to make out the figure.

The two friends finally got close enough to see it was an old Japanese lady. Her silver hair was an unkempt mess piled on top of her head. She walked with her back hunched over and her hands clasped behind her back. "Um...excuse me, old lady..." Eric waved her down.

"Eh?" The woman twisted sideways to look up at the

two tall foreigners approaching her. "What is it?" she replied in Japanese. Unfortunately neither Josh nor Eric knew much Japanese, and the old lady knew even less English.

"Have you seen any cameras around here?" Eric asked, hoping she'd at least recognize what they were looking for.

"*Ka-me-ra?*" the woman slowly repeated.

"Yeah!" Eric replied excitedly. "Camera!"

The woman made a loud cackling sound that echoed through the woods. It took a second for both Eric and Josh to realize the cracking, hollow sound was actually coming from the old woman. *"Yare, yare,"* she finally exclaimed, and pointed back down the road as part of the fog blew away, revealing a moss-covered stone gate.

"Over there? Oh, cool!" Eric said. He turned back to the old lady and gave her an awkward bow. "Thank you!"

Josh copied his friend's action, and they continued toward the gate. Two professional camcorders and one handheld camera were neatly lined up on the fourth step up from the ground.

"Dude, why does that creep me out even more?" Josh said quietly. He frowned and picked up one of the professional cameras. Although it was a bit scratched, it still powered on. "Looks like it works fine," he mumbled.

"Yeah, this one too," Eric replied. He was examining the other professional camcorder. A small red light blinked in the corner of the viewfinder, signaling that the battery was about to die. He switched off the device and glanced at the handheld camera. It was the one Mikey—and later, Dante

—had carried around. Out of the three, it was the most beat up. Eric leaned down and picked it up. He pressed the power button only to be met with a dead battery signal in the viewfinder. "This one has a dead battery," he told his friend.

"Now that we've found the cameras, can we get the hell out of here?" Josh asked through chattering teeth. "This place is giving me major spooky vibes!"

"Yeah, yeah." Eric laughed uncomfortably. He didn't want to admit he was afraid as well.

The Two Dingle Buds started their journey back to the *ryokan*. After a few moments of walking in silence, Eric looked at the small camera in his hand again. "I wonder if we should watch the footage?" he thought out loud.

"What?!" Josh glared at his friend. "And risk some *Ring*-level type shit cursing us? No fucking way, man!" He could never understand where Eric got his crazy, stupid ideas.

Eric made a disappointed click with his tongue. "You're no fun." He pouted then laughed. "I was curious if they caught footage of the *kappa* eating ass."

"Eric," Josh admonished his friend like a disappointed mother.

"I'm sorry," Eric whined in response. "You know humor is how I cope when I'm scared!"

"At least you finally admit it." Josh smiled. "Let's just get back and get rid of this footage."

For the past six years, Allison Park had been the main editor for Dante's channel. Any top VidTV content creator knew finding a good editor was just as important as any content they put out. An editor could make or break a video's popularity. Under Allie's editing, Dante's channel had nearly tripled in subscribers. She accentuated his entertaining humor with perfect comedic timing while trimming areas where he rambled. After all their time working together, Allie was usually comfortable with knowing what Dante wanted in his videos. Even his new venture into ghost hunting didn't pose a problem for her editing skills—that is, until she received the footage from Japan.

She had just received the digital footage files from Eric Ross of the Two Dingle Buds. The only message in the email was:

Hey. Dante asked us to send this to you. He said to post it when you're finished editing.

There was no explanation of what had happened to Dante and the crew, or why Dante didn't contact her himself, or how Two Dingle Buds had run into Dante. Shortly after Allie had received the footage, she had learned from the news that Dante was to remain in Japan to cooperate with a police investigation while also recovering from a broken foot, which could take four to six weeks to heal.

All the confusion left Allie with more questions than

answers. Due to the police being involved, Dante's phone had been confiscated for the time being. How long would Dante be stuck in Japan? When would she be able to contact him again? Where were Damien, Mike, Jen, and Andy? But most important, what the hell had happened in those woods? Allie got her answers to the last question when she went through the footage.

Things started off pretty normal. "Hello! Hellfiredante here back with another ghost-hunting video," Dante said in his intro. From the picture quality, Allie guessed the footage was from Mikey's handheld camera. In the video, Dante explained where they were, then told the ghost story of the innkeeper's daughter. Suddenly there was a loud thud in the woods, and things got weird. During the hike, the video caught several shadowy figures that peered out at the three men from behind moss-covered trees. Strangely neither Dante nor Damien reacted to any of these figures. It was almost as if they didn't see them.

The boys came into a clearing and the well came into view. A shiver ran down Allie's spine when she heard the fear in Damien's voice as he pleaded with Dante for them to leave the area. "Mate, this isn't a bit—I'm dead serious," he said urgently as the camera zoomed in on his frightened blue eyes. Allie had edited enough of Dante's videos to tell when Damien was playing along. This definitely was *not* a bit.

Finally Dante and Damien seemed to see one of the figures after a loud thud in the distance. The camera followed Dante as he raced off into the woods, but the video feed glitched and became fuzzy. "What the hell?" Allie mumbled, noting the minute mark where the video went bad. She waited for the static to clear and was about to move forward in the video. Then her hand froze when she heard it. There was the faint sound of incoherent whispering; then it grew louder. Allie turned her volume down, but the whispering became almost unbearably loud.

The video came back. Mikey must have been running over to Damien while carrying the camera. The two men continued to talk in hushed voices until Mikey noticed a moss-covered plaque. "Hey, Damien. Do you know what this says?" he asked.

As Damien explained it was a memorial, the whispering returned. This time it overlapped where Damien said the name, "It looks like her family name was Hikari..."

"Hikari," the whisper repeated clearly.

"But her first name is covered by moss," Damien continued. "It ends with –*ko*..."

"*Makiko desu*," the voice whispered in Japanese before switching to a clear Estuary accent similar to Damien's. "Nice to meet you, Allie."

Allie slammed the pause key on her keyboard and ripped her headphones off. She was inside her usually warm, comfortable office, but the temperature seemed to drop sharply. Her breath appeared in front of her in short white puffs. "Fuck this. I need a drink," she muttered, and left the room.

Several hours and several glasses of wine later, Allie emerged from her home office. It would take at least another week to try to edit the footage into a coherent video. She couldn't tell if the events were real or staged. If it was real, that made it all the more disturbing. Rather than continuing to waste time questioning if the contents of the footage was real, Allie decided to focus on her work. *Okay, Dante. I'll see what I can do.*

SIXTEEN
FIX IT IN POST

SEVEN DAYS *Later*

By herself, despite the creepy cursed shit she'd seen and heard while working on it, Allie managed to trim the four to five hours of combined footage to a compact forty-five-minute video. Exhausted, she decided to bring in a second pair of eyes for review before posting it.

"Was this staged?" asked Eddie Jaramillo, second editor for Dante's channel and Allie's assistant. His ADHD was evident as he played with a set of small magnets while swiveling back and forth in his office chair.

"I don't know," Allie replied flatly. Behind her large, round, hot pink, wire-rimmed glasses were dark under-eye circles. She hadn't been able to sleep peacefully for the past week; the image of the well in the video kept haunting her dreams. In each nightmare, she heard the whispering voice. It seemed to be counting down in Japanese... At least she thought it sounded like Japanese.

Eddie interrupted her thoughts. "What did you have to blur here?"

Allie blinked and noticed the video was already to where Dante and the others had found Mikey. It was another image that was haunting her. Jen's camera managed to capture the body face down in the stream with its partially eaten anus exposed to the night air before the video cut away. Andy's footage of the event was no better. It ended with the sound of him vomiting off-screen. "It was Mikey," Allie finally replied. "Some animals supposedly got him."

"Dude, that's messed up!" Eddie responded.

The two editors sat in silence as the rest of the video played out. They watched as one of the cameras seemed to hit the ground when Jen was screaming for help; Andy was running through the woods only to never appear again after his video stopped at a tree; and Dante discovered the lifeless body of his best friend in the shrine office. Finally, they watched the shaky footage of their boss trying to outrun a giant shadow. If the footage was staged, they did a fantastic job with the special effects. The video ended with Dante falling down the stairs and the video cutting to black.

"Wow!" Eddie whistled. "That's a hell of a cliff-hanger!" He turned his chair toward Allie. "This *has* to be fake, right?"

"I really don't know." Allie rubbed her eyes. "I only received the footage with the instructions to post it when we finished editing it."

"Hmm," Eddie hummed in thought. He tapped his finger against the desk, wondering if there was anything else that needed to be added. Suddenly he gasped. "Hey, what's this?"

"What?" Allie asked. The video already had ended. She wearily opened her eyes to see an image of the moss-covered well on the screen. It was the same image recurring in her nightmares. "What the hell? I didn't do this!"

"Stop playing! I'm not going to fall for it," Eddie replied.

"I'm serious!" Allie glared at him and pointed to the video progress bar, which continued to run after the total run time of forty-five minutes. "The video ended...or at least it should have."

"Then what the fuck is this shit then? Are you trying to curse me or something?" Eddie crossed himself while mumbling a prayer in Spanish.

Allie was about to reply when she was cut off by a whispering voice on the video. "Seven days..." It said ominously.

"Chingar!" Eddie cursed, nearly falling out of his chair as he pushed back away from the desk. Allie grabbed his left hand and steadied his chair by pulling him back toward her.

After a moment of silence, the sound of giggling erupted on the video. *"Ya, ya..."* Makiko walked into view on the video. She was doubled over with laughter. Allie and Eddie immediately recognized her delicate features. "Sorry," Makiko continued in the clear Estuary accent Allie had heard before. Makiko waved a hand at the camera. "I'm just kidding...or am I?"

Allie tried to hit the pause key, but Makiko continued to laugh. Next she tried to hit the stop key. No response. "Cut the power!" she ordered Eddie as she pointed to the power strip connected to her computer and monitors. Eddie followed her command and flipped the little red switch to "off" and yanked the power strip out of the socket.

"Aww! How cute," Makiko cooed on the screen. She clapped her hands together, long black claws clicking as they hit each other. The sound stopped Allie and Eddie in their tracks. "Let this serve as a warning to stay out of my forest," she coldly instructed her viewers. "Dante and his friends didn't listen. What they didn't realize is that *yokai* just act according to nature." She smirked. "I mean...would you expect a tiger to spare you when you stupidly walk into their den?"

"Stay out of the woods," she repeated. Then she pointed at the camera and said, "If not, I will see *you* in the next video." The two editors couldn't tell if it was a threat or promise. Makiko's eyes flashed a creepy magenta color. With a sweet smile, she waved at the camera and cheerily said, "*Jyaa ne*, bye-bye!" The screen turned dark as it completely turned off.

EPILOGUE
LIFE AFTER DEATH

SIX MONTHS *Later*

Dante exited his plane and navigated through the crowds of people at LAX to baggage claim. It was his first time back in Los Angeles since he'd originally left for Japan. While cooperating with the police investigation in Gifu, he was forbidden from any email, phone, or video contact with the outside world. The only person he saw aside from the police officers and medical personnel was his mom. Upon hearing that her son was involved in a police investigation, she immediately had gotten on a plane to help him.

Over the course of approximately five months, Japanese police combed the entire forest surrounding the Yamanaka Shinto Shrine and nearby Yamanaka Inn, searching for clues as to what had happened to Damien Knight, Michael Witt, Jennifer White, and Andrew Stein. Dante was initially their murder suspect, but any suspicions were ultimately dismissed due to lack of evidence.

Despite Dante's insistence that he and his friends were attacked, the police found nothing. Even when Dante tried to tell the police about Makiko, the Shinto priestess, he was informed that the shrine was generally unmanned for most of the year. There were no *yokai*, no *miko*, and no trace of the crew. It felt like he was being gaslighted.

"Hey, Mom." Dante nodded to his mother as he climbed into the passenger side of her sky-blue Prius. *"Tadaima,"* he added, remembering the Japanese greeting she had taught him for returning home.

"Okairi," she returned with a smile. "Welcome home," she said, translating her response into English for her son. "Is there anywhere you want to stop?"

"No. I just want to go home, please," Dante replied in a despondent voice. His downcast eyes expressed the stress he had faced over the last six months. "I'm going to take a short nap. Can you wake me up when we get to Brentwood?" Not wanting to pressure her son, Dante's mother nodded.

Thirty minutes later, Dante stepped into his house, dropped his luggage on the floor, and looked around the entrance in a daze. He should have felt relieved to be home. Instead, everywhere he looked, he was reminded of Jen, which then reminded him of Damien, Mikey, and Andy. His mind went into a frantic nosedive while he remembered the events from Japan. "Shit," he muttered, rubbing his forehead. Dark bags hung under his eyes, revealing how little he'd slept in the past six months. Cooperating in the police investigation had left him with no time to actually process the loss of his friends. Now that he was in the silent home he'd once shared with Jen, he felt how truly alone he was.

Staring blankly ahead, he didn't know what to do with himself. How was he supposed to move on with his life? It was his stupid idea that had gotten four of his closest friends killed. Dante let out a slow deep breath and finally came up with an idea. He swallowed his fear and went into the chat server app on his phone, which he shared with his team of editors. Ignoring all the messages he had received while in Japan, he immediately pinged his stream moderators.

In his office, he went to his desk, wiped the dust off both of his monitors, and switched on his computer. Although Dante wasn't known as a streamer, he felt the circumstances warranted an explanation to his fans. Aside from the scary viral video his editors had released six months ago on the *Dante's Inferno* VidTV channel, no one had heard from Dante. As his mods helped set up for the stream, Dante prepared to go live. It was second nature: Turn on ring light. Adjust mic. Check camera. Put on headphones.

A small red symbol showed up in his video feed, indicating he was recording live. He waited a minute or two for people to filter into his stream. Then he looked at the camera and began his usual boisterous intro. "Hello! Hellfiredante here...back...uh..." Dante's voice trailed off. His video introduction didn't feel appropriate.

Chat flashed by at an overwhelming speed. There were several comments accusing Dante's stream of being click bait or a stunt to get more subscribers. Others demanded to know where Damien was. The majority, however, expressed concern for Dante. "Look," he said, taking on a somber tone, "I know I disappeared six months ago." He frowned, but he insisted on doubling down on the truth and looked directly into the camera. "Let me tell you the story of what happened…"

<<<>>>

ABOUT THE AUTHOR

Emma Bowers is a first-time author leading a double life as a single mother and psychology doctoral learner. She studied and worked in Japan in the early 2000s, where she developed a love for Japanese language, history, arts, culture, and food. Currently she resides in the beautiful mountains of Northern New Mexico with her teenage son. When she's not writing or busy being a mom, she enjoys reading tarot, meditating, collecting crystals, and connecting with nature.

Printed in Great Britain
by Amazon